THE ZOM-B
CHRONICLES III

DARREN SHAN

THE

ZOM-B

CHRONICLES III

SIMON AND SCHUSTER

First published as an omnibus edition entitled ZOM-B CHRONICLES III
by Simon and Schuster UK Ltd in Great Britain in 2015
A CBS COMPANY

ZOM-B BABY first published in Great Britain in 2014
by Simon and Schuster UK Ltd
Text copyright © 2014 Darren Shan

ZOM-B GLADIATOR first published in Great Britain in 2014
by Simon and Schuster UK Ltd
Text copyright © 2014 Darren Shan

13 5 7 9 10 8 6 4 2

Simon & Schuster UK Ltd
1st Floor, 222 Gray's Inn Road
London WC1X 8HB

Simon & Schuster Australia, Sydney
Simon & Schuster India, New Delhi

A CIP catalogue record for this book
is available from the British Library.

Paperback ISBN: 978-1-47114-352-6
eBook ISBN: 978-1-47114-353-3

Printed and bound by CPI Group (UK) Ltd, Croydon, CR0 4YY

www.simonandschuster.co.uk
www.simonandschuster.com.au

THE ZOM-B

CHRONICLES III

ZOM-B BABY

For:
Mrs Shan!!!

OBE (Order of the Bloody Entrails) to:
Elisa Offord – queen of the mutant babies

Edited in a swanky city apartment by:
Venetia Gosling
Kate Sullivan

Darren Shan is represented by
the urban ladies and gentlemen
of the Christopher Little Agency

THEN . . .

When zombies rampaged through London on the day that the world fell, Becky Smith ended up trapped in her school. Having been cornered by the brain-hungry beasts, her heart was ripped from her chest and she became one of the living dead.

After months of mindless mayhem, she recovered her senses in an underground complex. She found out that there were two types of zombies — reviveds and revitaliseds. The latter could think and reason the way they had when they were alive, but they had to keep eating brains or they'd become hollow-minded reviveds again.

The revitalised teenagers in the complex referred to themselves as zom heads. They were being held prisoner by a group of scientists and soldiers. B hated being one of their lab rats, and refused to play along with their experiments. To punish her, they stopped feeding her, and she waited for her brain to shut down again.

Before B regressed, a nightmarish clown, Mr Dowling, invaded with a team of mutants, attacked the humans and freed the undead. B and another zom head called Rage managed to escape. B wandered the streets of London for a time, surviving on any scraps of brain that she could find in the many corpses littering the ruined city. During her travels she met an artist, Timothy Jackson, who believed God had set him the task of painting pictures of the zombies, so that future generations would have a record of the atrocities.

After another run-in with soldiers and the mutants, a broken, lonely B wound up at County Hall, where the centenarian Dr Oystein offered her refuge. He was one of the few adult revitaliseds in the world. The kindly scientist had established a base for undead, conscious teenagers like B. He referred to them as Angels and, like the artist Timothy, believed that he was on a mission from God.

Dr Oystein told B that he was the very first revitalised, that God had directly intervened to restore his senses, that he was working to save the world, under orders from the Almighty. As a baby, B had been vaccinated by one of Dr Oystein's nurses, as had all of the other revitaliseds. The vaccine was the reason they had recovered their senses.

But Dr Oystein hadn't saved the children to be charitable. He needed them to fight in a war. As B listened with a mixture of disbelief and horror, he told her that while he was an agent for a force of universal goodness, Mr Dowling was a being of universal evil. If the clown's army overcame Dr Oystein's Angels, the world would topple into a dark abyss and every survivor would fall prey to his foul, hellish servants.

NOW ...

ONE

The London Dungeon used to be one of the city's top tourist attractions. It was a fun but grisly place, a cross between a museum and a horror house. It recreated some of London's darker historical moments, bringing back to life the world of people like Jack the Ripper and Sweeney Todd. It featured sinister, imposing models of buildings from the past, props like hanging skeletons and snarling rats, nerve-tingling videos and light shows, and actors to play the various infamous figures. There were even some stomach-churning rides. I visited it quite a few times when I was alive, and always had a brilliant time.

I haven't been in the Dungeon since returning to County Hall as a revitalised, but right now it feels like the most natural part of the complex to head for.

I wander through the deserted rooms, enjoying the isolation and the gloominess. The actors are gone, and someone

9

must have done the rounds and turned off all the projectors and video clips, but most of the lights work, and the sets and props haven't been disturbed. It's still the coolest damn place in London.

I also think, looking back, that it served as a taste of what was to come. The London Dungeon painted a picture of a blood-drenched city full of terror and murder, and the people who built it were right — this *is* a realm of madness and death. We were never more than one sharp twist away from total chaos, from demonic clowns prancing through the streets and tender-hearted but loopy scientists setting themselves up as spokesmen for God.

I thought I'd escaped the craziness when I came to County Hall. London had been destroyed, zombies had taken over, life as we knew it had come to an end. But Dr Oystein seemed to offer sanctuary from the grim bedlam of the streets. I thought I could rest easy, make friends, learn from the good doctor, start to build a new life (or should that be *un*life?) for myself.

That was before the doctor told me that God speaks to him.

I creep along a street that looks like it's been transported to the present day from Victorian London. I pause, imagining banks of swirling fog, waiting for Jack the Ripper to leap out and claim me for his own. That's not very likely, I know, but it wouldn't surprise me. I reckon just about anything could happen in this crazy, messed-up world.

That's what's so weird and scary about the story Dr Oystein fed us. There was a time when I would have written him off as a crank, but given what I've seen and experienced recently, I can't say for sure that he *is* barking mad. He told me he was forced by Nazis to create the zombie gene — that's probably on the level. It's clear that he's an expert on the living dead, having studied them for decades. He's the one who gave me the ability to revitalise.

If all that and more is true, then why not the rest of it? The world has always been full of people claiming to be in contact with God. Surely they can't *all* have been nutters. If some of them were the genuine article, maybe Dr Oystein is too. The trouble is, how's an ordinary girl like me supposed to be able to tell the difference between a prophet and a madman?

I curse loudly and slam a fist into one of the fake walls, punching a large hole through it. Someone chuckles behind me.

'Now *there's* a cliché if ever I saw one.'

I turn and glare at Rage, who has followed me in from the riverbank. Mr Burke is with him. Rage is sneering. Burke just looks uncomfortable.

'Why don't you go drown yourself?' I snarl at Rage.

'I would if I could,' he smirks, then pokes his chest. 'I'm the same as you. My lungs don't work.'

I had left Rage, Burke and Dr Oystein abruptly, without

saying anything, once the doctor had hit us with the reve-lation that he was God's envoy, locked in battle with Mr Dowling, aka the literal spawn of Satan. I couldn't take any more. My head was bursting.

'I haven't been in this part of the building before,' Burke says, looking around.

'This was the London Dungeon,' I tell him.

My ex-teacher nods. 'I often meant to check it out, but I never got around to it.'

'I came here lots,' I sniff. 'My mum hated the place, but Dad was like me, he thought it was great. He'd bring me here, just the two of us, and we'd have a wicked time.'

'I bet,' Burke says.

'What's that supposed to mean?' I shout, thinking he's having a dig at my racist dad, implying that he liked the hor-rors of the Dungeon because he was horrific himself.

Burke blinks, startled by my tone. 'Nothing. It looks like it must have been a lot of fun back in the day. That's all I was saying.'

Rage snorts. 'Always thought the Dungeon was rubbish myself.'

I laugh shortly. 'That's because you're a moron with no taste.'

'Yeah,' he says. 'That must be why I fancy you.'

I give him the finger, but chuckle despite myself.

'So what do you think of old Oystein's story?' Rage asks.

I shrug and look away.

'He's off his head, isn't he?' Rage pushes.

'I suppose . . .'

'Do you think any of it was real? Being imprisoned by the Nazis, inventing the zombie gene, working with governments and armies all these years to suppress breakouts?'

'Those are undeniable facts,' Burke says quietly. 'I discussed Dr Oystein with my military contacts when I was leading a double life. Everything he told us today checked out.'

'What about his direct line to God?' Rage jeers.

Burke sighs. 'That's where we hit a grey area.'

'Nothing grey about it,' Rage says cheerfully. 'The doc's a lunatic. I don't believe in God, the Devil, reincarnation, nothing like that. Even if I did, his story doesn't ring true. The all-powerful creator of the universe teaming up with a brain-hungry zombie? Get real!'

'Many prophets were outcasts of their time,' Burke murmurs. 'They were mistrusted and feared by their contemporaries, mocked, abused, driven from their homes. Christ was crucified, John the Baptist's head was chopped off, Joan of Arc was burnt at the stake.'

'Yeah,' Rage says, 'but they were human, weren't they? They were alive.'

'Lazarus,' I say softly, the memory coming to me out of nowhere. 'Jesus raised him from the dead. The first zombie.'

Rage starts to laugh, then considers what I've said and frowns. 'You think the doc's telling the truth?'

I pull a face. 'How the hell do I know? It sounds crazy, but . . .'

'I don't do *buts*,' Rage says. 'It's a simple world as long as you don't let others complicate it for you. The doc's a genius, no one's denying that, but he's mad too. I respect him for the Groove Tubes, bringing the Angels together and all the rest, but I'm not gonna pretend there wasn't steam coming out of his ears when he started telling us about his cosy chats with God.'

'So what are you gonna do?' I ask.

'About what?'

'This war he wants us to fight. The Angels versus Mr Dowling and his army of mutants. If you don't believe God's on our side, or that we're fighting the forces of darkness, where does that leave you?'

'Right where I want to be,' Rage smirks. 'In the thick of it all.'

He walks up to the plasterboard wall I punched and studies the hole I made.

'We're built to fight,' he whispers, rubbing together the bones sticking out of his fingers. 'We were reborn as perfect killing machines. I always wanted to join an army. I had it all planned. I was gonna give myself a couple of years after school to see the world, have some laughs, sow my wild seeds.'

14

'Oats,' Burke corrects him.

'Whatever. Then I was gonna join the French Foreign Legion or something like that. Go where the battles were, test myself on the field of combat, maybe become a mercenary further down the line, hire myself out to whoever paid me the most.'

'You don't believe in loyalty to a cause?' Burke asks diplomatically.

'Loyalty's for mugs,' Rage says.

Burke looks disappointed. 'Then you're not going to stay with Dr Oystein?'

Rage frowns. 'Weren't you listening? I want to be where the action is. Dr Oystein's five cans short of a six-pack, but if he's gonna start a war with the clown and his mutants, I want to be there when they clash. So, yeah, I'm his man if he'll have me.'

'You're going to stay even though you think Dr Oystein is mad?' I gawp.

'Of course,' Rage says calmly. 'War's in my blood. I want to be a warrior and Oystein's offering me the best fight in town. Why would I turn my back on the chance to go toe to toe with an army of mutants and their diabolical leader? Hell, if we win, I might end up saving the world from the Devil — how ironic would that be, given that I don't even believe in the bugger?'

Rage turns to leave.

'And what if the Devil makes you a better offer?' Burke asks. Rage looks back uncertainly.

'What if Mr Dowling asks you to join him somewhere down the line?' Burke presses. 'Would you consider a proposal from our enemy?'

'Might do,' Rage nods. 'Offhand I can't think of anything he could offer to tempt me, since money doesn't mean anything these days. But never say never, right?'

'You'd sell us out?' I shout.

'In a heartbeat,' Rage says, then flashes his teeth in a merciless grin. 'God, the Devil, forces in-between . . . It makes no difference to me. I'll go where the going's good. Right now I'm best off sticking with Dr Oystein. But I'm not in this game to save the world or what's left of mankind. I'm just a guy in search of some kicks to pass the time before my tired old bones give up the ghost.'

Rage cocks his head and grunts. 'If the doc's right about us being able to survive for thousands of years, that's a lot of time to play with. I'll need a lot of kicks. Maybe spend a century working for the good guys, then a century for the villains. Or take on the whole lot of you together — Rage against the world. Wherever the opportunity for the most excitement lies, that's where you'll find me.

'Take care, folks. And watch your backs.'

Then, with a laugh, he's gone, leaving Burke and me to stare at each other in open-mouthed disbelief.

TWO

'Maybe you were right,' Burke mutters. 'We might have been better off if we'd killed him when he was in the Groove Tube.'

I chuckle. 'You don't really mean that.'

'No,' he smiles. 'I suppose I don't. But I'll have to keep a close watch on him. I hadn't realised he was this dangerous.'

'The clue was in the name,' I note drily.

Burke winces. 'It's always a dark day when the student becomes the teacher. Especially a student as limited as you were. No offence.'

'Get stuffed.'

We laugh, and for a while it's like we're back in school, just a cool teacher and a teenage girl sharing a joke.

'So what do *you* think of the whole Dr Oystein and God thing?' I ask.

Burke sighs. 'Does it matter?'

'Of course it does.'

'Why?' he challenges me. 'Isn't faith a personal choice? Don't we all listen to our hearts and choose to believe – or not – based on what we feel rather than on what other people tell us?'

'No,' I snort. 'We believe whatever our parents tell us, until we're old enough to decide for ourselves. Then most of us go along with what we grew up with because it's easier than trying to learn something new.'

Burke claps enthusiastically. 'My star student. Why did you never come up with airtight reasoning like that in class?'

'Because school was boring,' I tell him.

'Ouch,' he says, then sighs again. 'You're right of course. But whether we choose to believe or just stick with the faith we've grown up with, the truth is that nobody can ever say for sure if there's a God or not. Dr Oystein is convinced that there is, and for all I know he's right.'

'But if he's not?' I press.

'I don't think it matters.' Burke grimaces. 'I mean, under different circumstances I'd be wary of him. Lots of wars have been fought by people who used religion as an excuse. Kings, politicians and generals twisted the beliefs of their followers as they saw fit, playing the religious card to justify their crusades over land, oil, gold or whatever it was they were really fighting for.'

'Isn't that what Dr Oystein is doing?' I ask.

'I don't think so. He's asking us only to have faith in him, not in his God, to accept that he's working in the name of good, to overcome the forces of darkness which are stacked against us. Whatever you think about God, nobody can deny that we're facing dark times. The zombies, Mr Dowling and his mutants ... These are forces we can't ignore, enemies that have to be faced. Every so often a war that *must* be fought comes along, and I think this is one of them.'

'Yeah, fair enough,' I mumble. 'But is a nutjob the best man to lead the fight against the bad guys?'

'If not Dr Oystein, then who?' Burke asks. 'You?'

'Hell, no. I'm not a leader.'

'Nor am I,' Burke says. 'It takes a certain breed of person to command. Dr Oystein is a rarity, a man with the ability to lead but not the desire — he's told me that he's only doing this because it's him or nobody, and I believe him. The alternative is someone who craves power — the likes of Josh Massoglia or Dr Cerveris. Do you really want to pledge yourself to someone like that?'

'No, but ...' I shift uncomfortably. 'I didn't like Josh or Dr Cerveris, but they ran a tight ship.'

'Until Mr Dowling penetrated their defences,' Burke says, then leads me from the Victorian chamber, through the rest of the Dungeon, and out towards the front of the building.

When we're in the fresh air, beneath the shadow of the London Eye, he continues.

'This is a chance to start afresh,' he says softly. 'Whether it was divine retribution or a mess of our own making, the world *has* fallen, the old order *has* crashed and burnt. If we can find a way to deal with the zombies, this is an incredible opportunity to begin again and try to improve upon the mistakes of the past.

'If you believe the stories of the Old Testament in the Bible, this isn't the first time this has happened. The Flood wiped the slate clean and people had to start over. Things didn't work out too well that time, but who's to say we can't do better now? The zombies and mutants are clear-cut enemies. Everyone can recognise them as a threat and join against them — Jew, Christian, Muslim, Hindu, white and black, all fighting together, differences set aside.

'If we win this war, power-hungry people will immediately start thinking about how to establish control over the remnants of mankind. They'll look for new foes and threats, and work the survivors up into an agitated state. Hatred and domination are the ways of the past and will in all likelihood be the ways of the future too. Unless Dr Oystein and his Angels can help us change.'

Burke pulls a face. 'I know I'm being a crazy optimist, but I can't help myself. The best that the old leaders can offer is a return to the status quo. I think, based on what I've seen of him, that Dr Oystein holds the promise of true redemption. He's what a leader should be — a man who is reluctant to tell others how they should behave and what they should believe.'

'I don't know if I agree with you,' I say miserably. 'I want to, but I can't get over the fact that this is a guy who claims to be in touch with God. It's hard for me to go along with someone like that.'

Burke nods. 'I understand. I won't try to pressure you, just as Dr Oystein won't. If you can reconcile yourself to working with us, we'll welcome your support and you can help us take the fight to Mr Dowling, rescue survivors, work with those who've established compounds beyond the confines of the city, search for a way to suppress the zombies. There's going to be so much to do, so many wars to be waged. We'll need all the help we can get.

'But if you can't trust the doctor, we'll respect your decision. You're free to leave any time you want. I doubt you'll find a more secure home anywhere else in this ruin of a country, but if you need to search for one, you'll depart with our best wishes.'

I growl uncertainly. 'I want to stay with you, but I'm gonna need more time to think about it.'

'That's fine,' Burke says. 'We're in no rush. Take all the time you want.' He turns to leave, then looks back at me with a wicked twinkle in his eyes. 'You know what might help?'

'What?' I ask suspiciously.

Burke points to the sky. 'You could pray,' he says, then skips along with a laugh as I hurl a most unholy curse after him.

THREE

I head back to the training room and find Master Zhang
still there, sitting in a corner. He nods for me to enter
when he sees me in the doorway. I take up a position
opposite him. He's sitting cross-legged on the floor, but I
just plop down on my bum and draw my knees up to my
chest.

There's a sweet smell in the air. Some kind of flavoured
tea. It's coming from a pot to the master's right. There's a
kettle of water boiling on a small stove to his left.

'I miss the taste of tea more than anything,' he says softly,
lifting the lid of the pot to stir the contents. 'It was one of
the great pleasures of my life. I did not realise how important it was to me until I was denied it.'

Zhang sniffs the fumes then pours some more water into
the pot. He turns off the stove and leaves the kettle to cool.
There are some cups stacked behind him. He reaches back

slowly, picks up two, passes one to me and sets the other down in front of him.

'Is this a tea ceremony?' I ask.

'You know of such things?' He sounds surprised.

'I saw it on a few travel programmes. Looked like a lot of hassle for a simple cup of tea.'

'The tea ceremony is an ancient Japanese ritual,' Zhang says, pouring a cup of tea for me and one for himself. 'It has much more to do with etiquette and tradition than tea. It is a purification process for the soul, a way to honour your guests and bond with them.

'This is not a tea ceremony,' he says, picking up his cup and inhaling. 'I just enjoy the smell and the memory of the taste.'

Zhang sips from the cup, swishes the liquid round his mouth, then picks up a bowl which had been standing next to the cups and spits into it. He passes me the bowl and I follow suit, smelling the fumes, sipping the tea and spitting it out.

'Didn't get much of a kick from it,' I note.

'No,' he says sadly. 'This is a delicate blend. The flavours are subtle and difficult to detect even with an appreciative tongue. With our useless taste buds, we might as well be sipping water.'

'Then why bother?' I frown.

'We might not be able to dream,' Zhang says, 'but we can

use our imaginations. With the aid of the scent and the texture of the tea, I can sometimes trick myself into believing that I still taste.'

He takes another sip, swishes, spits it out and makes a sighing sound. 'This is not one of those days.'

We take a few more sips, pretending there's a point to this. The smell grows on me after a while, and sets me thinking about something.

'Why do you suppose we can smell when we can't taste?'

I'm not really expecting an answer, but Zhang surprises me.

'It is for practical reasons,' he says. 'Zombies need to smell, in order to be able to sniff out brains. But since brains are all we eat, we can function without our taste buds.'

I scratch my head, thinking it over. 'Yeah, that makes sense. I should have figured it out before.'

'Yes,' Zhang says. 'You should.'

I scowl, then laugh. 'You're Chinese, aren't you?' I ask, changing the subject.

'Yes.'

'But the tea ceremony is Japanese . . .'

'I have travelled widely,' he says. 'I like to think of myself as a citizen of the world. Besides, the Chinese introduced tea to Japan, so I feel that I have a natural entitlement to engage in the ceremony.'

'What's the situation like in China now?' I ask.

'Not good,' he says quietly. 'We had the largest population in the world. That means we now have the largest number of zombies. Life is grim everywhere for those who have survived, but it is particularly difficult in China and India.'

We finish off the tea in silence. When we're done, Zhang stands and moves to the centre of the room, beckoning me to follow. I stand opposite him, ready to be hurled to the floor. But this time he throws a punch at my face.

With a yelp, I knock his hand aside and step back. He follows, throwing another punch. Again I block it and move away from him. Zhang sweeps his leg beneath both of mine and I fall in a heap.

'What the hell!' I snap, rolling away from him.

'You blocked admirably,' he says calmly. 'And your first defensive step was well judged. Your second, on the other hand ...' He tuts.

I stand and dust myself down. 'Is this the start of my real training?' I ask.

'No,' he says. 'The real training started the first time I threw you.'

He chops at me and forces me back again. This time I repel four of his attacks before he sweeps my feet from under me.

'You know what I mean,' I mutter, rising again. 'Are you going to teach me to fight now, to strike and defend myself, the way you teach the others?'

'Yes,' he says and comes forward a third time, lifting his left foot high to kick my chest. I grab the leg and try to twist it. Zhang rolls with the twist, brings his right leg up and kicks the side of my head, knocking me to the ground.

'That was ambitious,' he says. 'Ambition is good. Caution is better, at least to begin with.'

'You're telling me to walk before I try to run?' I ask, getting up again.

'No,' he says. 'We have no time for walking here. You must learn swiftly and take short cuts. I do not have time to train you in all the ways of the martial arts. So, when in doubt, go for the simplest solution.'

Zhang kicks at me with his left foot again. This time I chop at his ankle then step back out of reach.

'Good,' he grunts and closes in, kicking, punching, chopping, forcing me back, testing my reflexes.

Zhang spars with me for half an hour before telling me to go and rest. 'You did well,' he says. 'We will focus on specific moves next time. This was a useful first workout.'

I bow to Master Zhang and turn to leave. But something's niggling me. I stop and face him again. He raises the eyebrow of his bloodshot eye – it must have been bloodshot when he was turned into a zombie, and since we don't heal properly, I'm guessing it will be like that forever – then nods to let me know I can speak.

'Did Dr Oystein tell you to do this?' I ask. 'To step up my training and stop just throwing me about?'

'Why would you think that?' he replies.

'Dr Oystein told me about his conversations with God.'

Zhang's expression doesn't change. He waits for me to continue.

'I think it's a load of nonsense. I'm not sure if I believe in God. Even if I do, I don't think He talks to zombies and asks them to save the world.'

'You must be a wise young lady to be able to dismiss the teachings and beliefs of your elders so easily,' Zhang says.

'Of course I'm not,' I say sourly. 'I know my limits. But my nose works as well as yours. I recognise bullshit when I smell it.'

'Really?' Zhang smiles thinly. 'Did you eat cheese when you were alive?'

I look at him as if he's crazy. 'What sort of a question is that?'

'A simple one. I enjoyed cheese very much and tried many varieties over the years. They all tasted good to me, but the smell ... Some smelled as good as they tasted. Others stank of old socks, fresh vomit, even, yes, *bullshit*.'

'Is this one of those famous Chinese riddles?' I ask when he doesn't continue.

'No,' he says. 'I am merely pointing out the fact that sometimes one cannot judge by smell alone. Oystein said nothing to me of his meeting with you. I decided to vary your routine because I thought the time was right. I will be doing the same with Rage when he next comes to me. There is nothing more to it than that, no matter what your nose might tell you.'

'Fair enough,' I grunt.

'You believe me?' he asks.

'Yeah.'

'Then why don't you believe Oystein?'

'Because you're not telling me that you can talk with God.' I pause. 'You're not, are you?'

Zhang shakes his head. 'I do not believe in God. Or reincarnation. Or any kind of supernatural realm.' He makes a small sighing sound, looking his age for once — he can only have been in his early twenties when he was turned into a zombie. 'My lack of faith was a source of grave concern for my parents.'

'Then what the hell are you doing here?' I growl.

He shrugs. 'I believe in the doctor. He rescued me years ago. I was living in a small village but had moved there from a large city. I had been vaccinated against the zombie gene. Oystein kept track of me, the way he tried to keep track of all his children — and that is how he thinks of us.

'When there was an outbreak of zombies in my village, troops moved in to contain it. We were sealed off from the world and those who had been infected were executed.

Oystein made sure that I was not killed. He had me isolated and fed. My guardians were issued with strict instructions not to harm me.

'I took almost five months to revitalise. Most people would have given up on me. Not Oystein. He hates abandoning any of us.'

'But it's got to be a problem for you,' I mutter. 'How can you believe in him if you don't believe he really speaks with God?'

'It is not an issue,' Zhang insists. 'He has never asked me to accept his beliefs. He has only asked me to fight, which is all he is asking of you too.'

Zhang returns to his cups and bowls and begins to tidy them away. 'It is very straightforward in my view,' he says. 'A war to decide the future of this planet is being fought. We must choose sides or pretend it is not happening. Assuming you do not go down the road of blind ignorance, and are not on the side of evil, you must back Oystein, regardless of whatever flaws you perceive in him, or look for another leader to support.'

'Do you think there are others out there?'

'I am sure there are. But they will have flaws too. You must ask yourself which is worse — a leader firmly rooted in reality who thirsts for power and control, or a truly good-hearted man who might be a touch delusional.

'I do not think that God exists,' Zhang says, heading for

the door. 'But there are certainly godly people on this planet, and I am honoured that one of them has deemed me worthy of his friendship and support. You should be too, as I doubt there are many pure people in this world who would see goodness within *you*.' He looks at me with a probing expression. 'Do you even see it within yourself?'

I think of the bad things I have done. Of my racist past. Of Tyler Bayor.

And I can't say a word.

'I will see you tomorrow for training,' Zhang says softly, and shuts the door with a heel, leaving me even more confused and unsure than I was when I came in.

FOUR

I head back to my room, taking my time, creeping through the deserted corridors of County Hall, thinking about all that I've been told. As I'm passing one of the building's many chambers, I hear a strange moaning noise. I slow down and the noise comes again. It sounds like someone in pain. Worried, I open the door. The room is pitch-black.

'Hello?' I call out nervously, wary of a trap.

'Who's that?' a girl snaps.

'B,' I reply, relaxing now that I've placed the voice.

There's a pause. Then the girl says, 'Come in and close the door.'

Shutting the door behind me, I shuffle forward into darkness. I'm about to ask for directions when a dim light is switched on. I spot the twins, Awnya and Cian, in a corner. Awnya is sitting against a wall. Cian is lying on the floor, his head buried in his sister's lap. He's trembling and moaning into his hands, which are covering his face. Awnya is stroking the back of her brother's head with one hand, holding a small torch with the other.

I cross the room and squat beside Awnya. 'What's going on?' I whisper as Cian makes a low-pitched weeping noise, his body shaking violently. 'Is he sick?'

'Only sick of this world,' Awnya says quietly. She looks at me with a pained expression. 'We often come to a quiet place like this. We feel so lonely and we've seen so many horrors ... Sometimes it gets too much for us and we have to break down and cry.'

'Zombies can't cry,' I remind her.

'Not the normal way,' she agrees, 'but we can cry in our own fashion.' She strokes Cian's head again. 'We take it in turns to comfort one another. We can't both break down at the same time or we might never recover. One of us always looks out for the other.'

Cian starts to gibber nonsense sentences, then he curses and whimpers. Awnya lays down her torch, massages his shoulders with both hands and sings to him, an old ballad which I vaguely recognise. It should be laughable but it's strangely touching.

'Do you want me to leave?' I whisper between verses.

'Not unless you feel awkward,' Awnya says and carries on singing.

I lay my head against the wall and listen to the song. I'd

like to close my eyes but I can't. Instead I study the shadows thrown across the room by the torch. There are cobwebs running along the top of the skirting board opposite us. The world has gone to hell, but life goes on as usual for these spiders. They know nothing of zombies, mutants, God. They just spin their webs and wait for dinner. Lucky sods.

Cian eventually stops snivelling and sits up. He rubs his cheeks and smiles shakily at me, embarrassed but not mortified.

'We're lucky,' Awnya says, brushing Cian's blond hair out of his eyes. 'We have each other. I don't know how the rest of you cope.'

I shrug. 'You learn to deal with it.'

'It's because we're the youngest,' Cian mutters. 'Dr Oystein says that a year or two makes a big difference. He says we can go to him any time we want, for comfort or anything else, but he thinks it's better if we can support ourselves.'

'This is a hard world for the weak,' Awnya notes.

'We're not *weak*,' Cian snaps.

Awnya rolls her eyes, then squints at me. 'Did Dr Oystein tell you everything?'

'Yeah.'

'It's brilliant, isn't it?' Cian says. 'Being on the side of God and all.'

'I think it's scary,' Awnya murmurs.

'That's because you're a girl. Girls are soft,' Cian sniffs, apparently forgetting that moments earlier he was whining like a baby. 'I'm not afraid of the Devil, Mr Dowling or anyone else.'

'Of course you are,' Awnya says. 'We all are. And we're right to be afraid, aren't we, B? You met the clown. He's as scary as Dr Oystein says, isn't he?'

I nod slowly. 'He's a terrifying bugger, there's no doubt about that. But as for him working for the Devil, don't make me laugh.'

'What do you mean?' Awnya asks.

'You don't really believe that, do you, about God and the Devil?'

'Of course we do,' Cian says stiffly. 'Dr Oystein told us.'

'And you buy everything he says?' I sneer.

'Yes, actually,' Awnya growls, pushing herself away from me.

'Dr Oystein saved us,' Cian says.

'He gave us a home,' Awnya says.

'He's a saint,' Cian says.

'Our only hope for the future,' Awnya says.

'Yeah, yeah,' I rumble. 'He's doing a fantastic job and he's a first-rate geezer, but that doesn't change the fact that he's crazy. If God is real, He doesn't get involved in our affairs. This is all about what our stupid scientists and armies have done to the world, not about a war between God and Satan.'

'Hmm,' Awnya says, pretending to think hard. 'Who should I trust? A genius who's been working for decades to try and save mankind, or a girl with a chip on her shoulder?'

'What chip?' I grunt.

'I don't know,' Awnya says. 'But you must have one, otherwise why are you saying nasty things about Dr Oystein? You've only been here five minutes, yet you're telling us we're stupid, that we should listen to you instead of the man who loves and protects us.'

'I'm just saying it's madness,' I whisper.

'Dr Oystein's maybe the only person in this world who *isn't* mad,' Cian huffs. 'God spoke to him, touched him, changed him. He's the best of us all.'

'You really believe that?'

'Yes,' Cian says.

'Absolutely,' Awnya says.

'One hundred per cent,' Cian adds, in case there's any doubt.

'Fine,' I shrug and get to my feet. 'I wish I could believe it too. I'm not trying to stir things up. I just can't see it. I want to but I can't.'

'Then you're in an even worse state than us,' Awnya says and there's genuine sympathy in her tone.

'Yeah,' I say hollowly. 'I guess I am.'

I start for the door but Awnya stops me. 'B?' I look back

at her questioningly. 'If it's any comfort, we're jealous of you.'

'Why?' I frown.

'Dr Oystein and Master Zhang chose you to fight,' she says.

'They didn't pick us,' Cian says glumly.

'Dr Oystein loves us all,' Awnya says, 'but even though I'm sure he'd deny it, he's got to love his warriors more than the likes of Cian and me. You're the ones who are going to defeat Mr Dowling and save the world.'

'We're just the guys who find things for the rest of you,' Cian says.

'If we could swap places with you, we would,' Awnya says.

I scratch my head while I think that over. 'You two are a couple of freaks,' I finally mumble. We all laugh — they know I meant it in a nice way. Cian and Awnya wave politely at me. I flip them a friendly finger then let myself out.

FIVE

All of my room-mates are present when I get to my bed-room, including Rage, who's studying Ashtat's model of the Houses of Parliament.

'It's all matchsticks?' he's asking.

'Yes,' Ashtat says.

'There isn't a ready-made frame underneath that you've stuck them on to?'

'No, it is all my own work.'

'Cool.'

Ashtat smiles sappily and tugs shyly at her white head-scarf.

'You want to be careful,' I call to her, 'or he'll burn the bugger down.'

Rage grins. 'Don't say such nasty things about me, Becky. I want to make a good impression on my new friends.'

'You don't have any friends here,' I snort.

38

'Isn't that for us to decide?' Ashtat snaps.

'She's got a point,' Carl says. 'We know you don't like this guy, but that doesn't mean the rest of us have to hate him.'

'Yeah,' Shane grunts. 'He seems all right to me.'

'He's a killer,' I growl. 'I saw him murder a man.'

'She's got me bang to rights,' Rage says chirpily as the others stare at him. 'I can't deny it. Guilty as charged, officer.'

Rage swaggers over to his bed and sits on it, testing the springs.

'What Miss Smith *might* have failed to mention,' he adds, 'was that I'd been kept captive and denied brains for several days, which meant I was close to reverting and becoming a mindless revived. The man I killed had imprisoned and starved me. In my eyes that made him fair game.'

'The rest of us had been starved too,' I snarl. 'We didn't turn into killers.'

'As I recall, you were quite keen to tuck into Dr Cerveris's brain once I'd cut open his skull,' Rage notes. 'If I hadn't stopped you, you'd have torn in like a pig at feeding time.'

'Maybe,' I concede. 'But I didn't kill him. You were the only one of us who killed.'

'Really?' Rage starts looking around as if searching for something. He even bends and peers under the bed. 'Where's Mark?' he finally asks.

'Bastard,' I sneer.

'Reilly told me what happened,' Rage chuckles. 'Your lot found out Mark was alive and you tore the poor sod apart. True or false?'

'The others did. Not me.'

'You abstained?'

'Yeah.'

'Then you have my respect,' Rage says quietly, his smile fading. 'You were able to control yourself. You're a better person than I am. Better than any of the zom heads were. But will you look down your nose at those of us who are made of weaker material?'

I stare at Rage uncomfortably. I didn't expect the argument to go like this. He was supposed to fight his corner, not praise me and make me feel bad for insulting him.

'I'm not proud of what I did in that hellhole,' Rage says. 'But I was in bad shape. I needed brains. If it hadn't been Dr Cerveris, if it had been someone good and decent, would I have killed them anyway? I like to think not, but I can't say for sure.'

I gulp – old habits die hard – and try to think of something to say, but I can't.

'All this honesty,' Rage says, grinning again. 'I never knew how invigorating it would make me feel to tell the truth all the time. You should try it, Becky. A bit of honesty's good for the soul.'

'I can be as honest as anyone,' I shout. 'I hate your guts

and always will, no matter what you say or do. How honest is that?'

'Good enough for me,' Rage laughs, cocking his head swiftly to the side, the closest any of us living dead can get to a wink.

I stomp to my bed, throw myself down and glare at the ceiling. A few minutes later, Carl comes and sits beside me. He's changed his clothes again, choosing an old-fashioned suit that looks plain wrong on a guy his age. He's brushed his dark hair back too, gelling it flat the way businessmen used to in old movies that I sometimes watched with my dad on a lazy Sunday. All he needs is a bowler hat and a fancy umbrella and he could be a fresh-faced banker from fifty or sixty years ago.

'How are you feeling?' he asks softly.

'Sick to my back teeth at having to share a room with *him*,' I snap.

'I meant about the rest of it, what Dr Oystein told you.'

I prop myself on one elbow and squint at Carl, who looks a bit sheepish.

'It can be hard to take it all in when he first tells you,' Carl continues. 'I was in shock for a few days. There's so much to think about and process.'

'You don't believe either,' I whisper. 'You think he's mad.'

'Who's that?' Rage pipes up. 'The doc? You can bet your sorry excuse for a life that he is. Mad as a hatter.'

'You shouldn't say things like that,' Shane barks.

'Why not?' Rage shrugs. 'It's what I think, how I feel. The doc won't mind. He has bigger things to worry about than whether or not the likes of us think he's the Messiah or a howling maniac.' He looks around at everyone. 'Come on, how many of you really believe that he speaks with God?'

Ashtat and Shane stick up their hands immediately. Jakob starts to raise his, wincing at the pain as he lifts his thin, skeletal arm, but then he stops and shakes his head. 'I don't know,' he croaks.

Carl keeps his hands on his knees. He looks troubled.

'Three against three,' Rage beams. 'Sounds about right to me. This world has always split down the middle when it comes to gurus. One man's prophet is another man's crackpot.'

'The difference here,' I mutter, 'is that those who doubt don't usually throw themselves behind the lunatics.'

'Of course they do,' Rage says. 'People pick their religion for all sorts of selfish, unspiritual reasons. We don't choose our holy men just because we think they'll sort us out when we die and our souls move on — we like to get some benefit from them in this life too.'

'I can see now why B doesn't like you,' Carl sniffs. 'You're a real cynic.'

'It's my best quality,' Rage smirks. 'But you're the same. Why are you trailing around after the doc if you don't believe he speaks with God? No need to answer. I know already. He's good for you. He set you up in this swanky spot, provides you with brains, trains you to fight. You'd have to be crazy to walk away from a cushy number like this. If the only downside of that is having to swallow his *I am the Right Hand of God* rubbish, well, that's an easy enough sacrifice to make. Am I right or am I right?'

'You think you're clever, don't you?' Carl growls.

'I do, actually, yeah,' Rage chuckles, then gets up and walks over to the foot of my bed. He stares down at me as I glare up at him. 'What's your problem?' Rage asks and he sounds genuinely curious. 'You've a face like a slapped arse. Why can't you just take the doc's out-there beliefs with a pinch of salt and go along for the ride like everyone else?'

'It's not that simple,' I mumble.

'Of course it is,' Rage says. 'All you have to do is hold your tongue when the doc's warbling on about heavenly missions. How hard can that be? In fact I bet he doesn't mention it that often. Am I right, Clay?'

Carl nods. 'He's barely mentioned religion to me since that first time. In fact he even apologises on the rare occasions when he namechecks God, since he knows that makes some people feel uncomfortable.'

'See?' Rage beams. 'Simple, like I told you.'

'It's not!' I shout, pushing Carl away and getting to my feet. I think about picking a fight with Rage but I don't. And it's not just because I know he'd wipe the floor with me. He's trying to help. He deserves an answer, not an angry retort.

'It's because of my dad,' I say sadly, sinking back on to my bed. 'He wasn't a nice guy. He used to beat me and my mum, and he was a racist. He made me do something even worse than what Rage and the other zom heads did underground ...'

I spill my guts, telling them everything, about Dad, how he campaigned to keep England white, the way he pressured me to copy his lead, how I went along with him for the sake of a quiet life. I end with what happened to Tyler Bayor, Dad screaming at me to throw him to the zombies, obeying because it was what I'd become accustomed to.

I choke up towards the end. I'd cry if I could, but of course the tears aren't there and never will be again. Still, my chest heaves and my voice shakes. I even let rip with a few involuntary moans, like Cian a while earlier.

There's a long silence when I finish. Everyone's looking at me, but I don't glance up to check whether they're staring with sympathy or loathing.

'I knew my dad for what he was,' I moan. 'A nasty sod, a bully, a manipulator. In the end, a monster. But I loved him anyway. I still do. If he walked in now, I'd hug him and tell him how much I've missed him, and it would be true. He was my father, whatever his faults.'

I get up and wander across the room to the model of the Houses of Parliament which Ashtat has been working on. I stare at it, gathering my thoughts.

'People complained about politicians in the old days, called them self-serving, greedy, power-hungry gits. But hardly anyone tried to change the system. They were our elected leaders and we felt like we had to go along with them because there was no other way.

'I did that with my dad and it was wrong, just as people were wrong to put up with the political creeps. There's *always* another way. If it's not clear-cut, we have to work hard to find it. We shouldn't trudge along, putting our faith in people who don't deserve it, accepting things because we're afraid of what will happen if we break ranks and try to build something better.

'Dad was a good man in certain ways. He was loyal to his friends. I don't think he ever cheated on Mum. He was brave — he risked his life to try and save me when the zombies attacked. But he thought that whites were superior to other races. It was a huge flaw in him. I could see it, but I put up with it because I didn't dare confront him.'

I turn away from the model and face the others. 'Dr Oystein's like my dad. A good man in many ways, but too sure of himself and the way the world should be ordered. I can't believe that God spoke to him. That doesn't seem to be an issue for Rage and Carl, but it is for me. Because I've seen what happens when you put your trust in people like that. They break your heart.' I tug at the material of my T-shirt and grimace. 'Some of the buggers even rip it from your chest.'

Then I go and lie down and stare at the ceiling and don't say anything else for the rest of the night.

SIX

I train hard for the next week. Now that Master Zhang has started practising proper moves with me, I learn new things every day. It's a real mix — karate, judo, boxing. We also focus a lot on fighting with knives, steel bars, hammers, screwdrivers, things like that.

'This is all about practical application,' he tells me. 'Apart from some knives, we will not send you out armed. You will fight mostly with your hands, but if you ever need a weapon, you must know how to make use of whatever you can find.'

I ask him why we don't use guns. 'The zombies don't have any. Surely we could just go out with rifles and mow them down.'

'There would be no honour in that,' he replies.

'But isn't this all about winning?' I press.

'Not at any cost,' he says. 'Oystein is adamant about that.

47

If we are to build a better world, we cannot do so by relying on the barbaric ways of the past.'

'Reilly has a taser,' I note.

'Reilly is human,' Zhang says calmly. 'We are not. We have a choice — we can be less than we were or we can try to be more.'

'It would be a lot easier if we had guns,' I mutter.

'The easy way is not always the better way,' he says. 'If we wish to rise above our foul situation, we must work harder to be honourable in death than we ever had to in life.'

Zhang shows me how to most effectively sharpen the bones sticking out of my fingers and toes. He says they're our best weapons and he teaches me how to incorporate them into the moves, how to dig and slice and gouge.

He also trains me to file my teeth in a different way. 'You never know when you might have to rip out someone's throat or chew through to their brain in a hurry.'

'Is there honour in biting open a person's throat?' I ask innocently.

'Less of your backchat,' he growls but I know he's smirking inside. We get along all right. We're similar in many ways. Tough nuts.

I don't discuss Dr Oystein with the other Angels. In fact I don't talk to them much at all. I've been brooding ever since that day in the aquarium. No matter which way I look at it, I can't accept what the doc told me. And being unable to accept that he's on a mission from God, I find it hard to accept anything else about him, his offer of refuge or a role in the war he's waging. Rage and Carl are able to sweep their misgivings under the carpet. I can't.

Rage is fitting in better than me. He's in his element, training hard with Master Zhang, messing about with our room-mates, getting to know other Angels. He's taken to this with ease.

That pisses me off. I was sure that Rage would be the outcast here, the one that the others would be wary of. I was almost looking forward to the day when he betrayed us, so I could say, 'Told you so!' But, as things stand, I'm the one who doesn't belong, who's falling adrift a little further every day. It's not that the others aren't trying to be nice to me. They are. But I see them as stooges who are playing along with Dr Oystein for all the wrong reasons, so I feel awkward around them and keep pushing them away.

The worst thing is, there's no one for me to confide in. I've seen Dr Oystein a few times over the week, in corridors, the dining room and gym. He's always smiled at me, made small talk a few times. I'm sure he'd be happy to discuss my concerns if I approached him, but what could I say? 'Sorry, doc, I think you're crazy and dangerous. Other than that you're OK.'

Mr Burke is the only person I'd feel comfortable chatting about this with, but he's gone off again on a mission, to infiltrate another complex like the one where I was held captive, or to spy on Mr Dowling, or ...

Actually, I don't know what Burke, Dr Oystein and the others get up to. There hasn't been much talk of how we're supposed to take the fight to Mr Dowling and his mutants. Things seem to operate on a need-to-know basis around here. Or maybe it's on an *if-we-can-trust-her* basis. Perhaps they're withholding information from me because they sense that I'm not fully committed.

I suppose that's logical. You don't want to share all your secrets with someone who might walk out the door at any given moment. In their position I wouldn't be too forth-coming with someone like me either. Still, that doesn't make life any easier, just increases my belief that it's me against the rest of them. Roll on full-blown paranoia!

'Oh, this is ridiculous,' I snap and push myself away from the table.

I'm in the dining room, having just tucked into a bowl of Ciara's latest batch of cranial stew. The others are still chewing. They stare at me uncertainly, surprised by my outburst.

'What's wrong?' Ciara asks, having stayed to chat with Reilly, who's munching a hamburger that I'd give my left ear to be able to taste. 'Is it too hot? Too cold? Lumpy?'

'I wasn't talking about the food.' I force a smile, not wanting to offend the sweet, fashionably-dressed dinner lady. 'The food's great. Honest. I just ... I can't deal with this any more. I've got to get some air. I'm going for a walk. I'll be back later.'

I storm away. I don't know why things should have come to a head here, now, but they have. Something inside me snapped when I was sitting at the table, thinking about Dr Oystein and his claim to have a link to a higher power, and how everyone is happy to go along with whatever the doc says. I've been playing the good little girl, saying nothing, but I can't do it any more.

I'm tramping down a corridor, not sure where I'm going or what my plans are, when someone rushes up behind me. Before I can react, arms snake across my stomach and grab me. I'm hauled into the air and twirled round. I catch a glimpse of Rage's face as I'm whirling.

'Let me go!' I shout.

'Your wish is my command,' he says and instantly releases me.

I stagger across the floor, slam into a wall and fall. My head is spinning badly. I lean forward and dry-heave. There are white flashes in front of my eyes.

'Are you all right?' Rage asks.

'No,' I gasp, then sit back against the wall and wait for my head to clear. When it finally does and the heaving stops, I glare at him. 'What did you do that for?'

'Just trying to cheer you up. Did you get dizzy?'

'What does it look like, numbnuts?'

'Did that used to happen when you were spun around in the past?' he asks.

'Yeah. Not as bad as this, but my ears were never the best. They used to pop like mad when I flew. If I went on a spinning ride at a funfair, I'd have a headache for hours.'

'Oh. I thought it might be something to do with being dead. I was worried for a minute.'

'No need to be,' I snarl, getting to my feet. 'You can still go on merry-go-rounds any time you like.'

'I preferred you when you were suffering,' Rage sniffs and reaches out to grab me again.

'You'll lose both hands if you try it,' I snap, then squint at him. 'Why the hell are you trying to cheer me up anyway? What does it matter to you how I feel?'

'It doesn't,' he says. 'But the others thought someone should come after you. They were concerned, thought you might do something stupid, maybe top yourself. I figured I'd look like a caring, sensitive guy if I volunteered to help you, especially as they all know that you hate me. So here I am.'

'You're too sweet for this world,' I jeer. 'Head on back to those muppets and tell them I'm fine.'

'Not yet,' Rage says. 'It's too soon. It wouldn't look like I'd tried very hard. I'll tag along with you for a while.'

'What if I don't want you to?'

'Tough.' He flashes me a grin. 'If you do want to top

yourself, I know a place where you can get some great power drills. I'll even help you choose the best bit for it. I'd love to see someone drill through their own skull.'

'There's the Rage I know and loathe,' I chuckle.

'*Honest Rage*,' he smirks. 'That's how I define myself these days. Telling the truth is what I'm all about.'

'It must be a nice change,' I sneer.

'It is.' There's a long silence while we eye each other. 'But seriously,' Rage says, breaking it, 'if you *do* want me to recommend a good drill . . .'

SEVEN

We exit County Hall and walk to the corner of the building. We can see part of Waterloo Station from here, and the London Eye.

'Have you been back into the station since Zhang tested us?' Rage asks.

I look at him oddly. 'No. Why the hell would I?'

'I have,' he says. 'I've gone in there with a rucksack seeded with brains, done the run through the zombies again, trying to improve my time.'

'Why?' I frown.

'I want to be top dog. You've got to push yourself if you want to get ahead.'

'You'd better be careful,' I say drily, 'or you'll wear yourself out.'

'Nah,' Rage grins. 'It's not just all about the training. I make time for fun stuff too. For instance, I walked up to the

IMAX theatre the other day. Wanted to see if I could screen a film.'

'Could you?' I ask.

'Wasn't able to try. The place was packed with zombies. I forced my way through to the projectionist's booth, but the buggers had beaten me to it. Some of them had made it their home and it was a mess, equipment smashed to pieces. A shame. I was hoping to screen *Night of the Living Dead* there.'

It's hard to tell if he's joking or not.

'The noise would have been awful anyway,' I note. 'The IMAX had the best sound system in London, great for a living person with normal hearing, but with ears like ours it would have been deafening.'

'Yeah,' Rage says. 'But fun. The reviveds would have hated it. They'd have howled like wolves.' He stretches, looks at the sky and grimaces. It's a cloudy day but still way too bright for the likes of us. 'Where were you headed before I stopped you?'

'Nowhere.'

'Really? You were marching like a girl with a purpose.'

'I just wanted to get away.'

Rage scratches an armpit and grunts. Must be force of habit — we don't sweat, so he can't have itchy pits.

'It's boring here, isn't it?' he says. 'That's why I keep look-ing for things to do. I hate the silence. A city should be buzzing, not quiet like this. It's like the God-awful countryside these days.'

'Nothing wrong with the countryside,' I sniff. 'I used to enjoy days out.'

'No, you didn't,' Rage argues. 'It was hell out there, nothing but fields, trees and Mother bloody Nature. If people loved that so much, they wouldn't have built cities and moved to them. The countryside's boring and so's London now.'

He turns in a circle, looking for something to amuse him. He pauses when he spots the London Eye, then nods at me. 'Come on.'

'I'm not going on the Eye. I've been up a few times since I moved into County Hall. It always leaves me feeling down, seeing how much of the city has been ruined.'

'Just follow me,' he insists.

At the Eye, instead of hopping aboard one of the pods, he heads for the control booth. There's always an Angel on watch in a pod, as well as one in the booth to monitor the big wheel. Today the person on duty is Ivor, a guy I know pretty well, although I wouldn't claim to be a close friend. I first ran into him when he was on a mission with his team, and we've had a few conversations since then, when our paths have crossed.

Ivor has brought a load of locks with him, and is fiddling with them to while away the time. He's able to pick just about any lock. I'd love to be able to do that, but although I've tried a few times, I'm not a natural.

'Don't you ever stop practising?' Rage shouts, startling Ivor, who was focused on the locks and didn't see us approach. He almost drops the lock that he's working on, but catches it just in time.

'It's good to keep your hand in,' Ivor says, smiling at us. 'My fingers are like a lock — they get rusty if I don't keep using them.'

Ivor spends a few minutes showing us how to pick the lock. He makes it look so easy, but I get nowhere with it. Rage doesn't even try.

'These fingers weren't made for work like that,' he says, giving them a wiggle.

'They're like sausages,' I laugh.

'Yeah,' he says. 'Perfect for smashing, not picking.'

We chat with Ivor for a while, then Rage asks if he can stop the Eye.

'Stop it?' Ivor frowns.

'Just for ten or fifteen minutes. You don't mind, do you?'

'I'm not supposed to,' Ivor says. 'Dr Oystein likes us to keep it going all the time.'

'I know. But we'll pretend that someone in a wheelchair was boarding and they got stuck.'

Ivor laughs. Rage works on him a bit more and finally he agrees to the odd request.

'But no more than a quarter of an hour,' he insists. 'And if the doc or Master Zhang asks, I'll tell them it was for you.'

'Cheers,' Rage says, hurrying out of the booth.

'What are you up to?' I ask suspiciously as I follow him.

'You'll see in a sec,' he promises and trots to the nearest pod.

There are small handles running around the pod. Rage grabs hold and climbs quickly until he's standing on the roof. I still don't know what he's planning, but I'm curious, so I climb up after him.

'They must be the biggest spokes in the world,' Rage says, staring at the mesh of links above us. 'Imagine if you had another wheel the size of this and you could make a bike out of them.'

'You're crazy,' I laugh.

'Yeah,' he grins, then jumps and grabs hold of one of the bars. He pulls himself up then slides across until he's hugging the rim of the wheel. 'Race you.'

'What?'

'Race you,' he beams. 'Come on, up you get.'

I stare at him uncertainly.

'Are you chicken?' he growls.

'Sod you,' I snap. 'I just don't know what you're talking about.'

'A race,' he says. 'Along the inside of the rim, all the way to the top.'

I frown, then study the metal rim. I follow it with my gaze at it curves outwards and upwards, before arcing back in on itself past the halfway mark and coming full circle at the top.

'You *are* bloody crazy!' I gasp, seeing now what he wants to do.

'I might be crazy but I'm no coward,' Rage chuckles. 'Come on, I dare you — a race. We're stronger than we were. We've got these neat bones sticking out of our fingers and toes to help us grip. I'm sure we can do it.'

'Even if we could, why the hell would we want to?'

'Now who's the crazy one?' he jeers. 'I'm challenging you to a race up the London Eye. Nobody could have done that in the past, not without equipment. How cool will it be to be the first pair in the world to free-climb this baby?'

'It's impossible,' I mumble. 'If we made it past the halfway point, we'd have to hang upside down.' I point to the bar running up the centre of the Eye, linking the two rims of the wheel. Smaller bars from the rims connect with it at regular intervals. We could use them for support. 'What about that way? It would be safer and easier.'

'This isn't about safe and easy,' Rage says. 'I think we'll be all right even if we fall – we're hard to kill – but if not, what of it? We've all got to go eventually. How would you prefer to leave this world — as a decaying, decrepit old fart, or trying to climb the London Eye in your prime?'

'Dr Oystein won't like it if a couple of his precious Angels risk their lives on something this pointless,' I murmur with a wicked smirk.

'I don't think either one of us is that bothered about keeping Dr Oystein happy,' Rage snorts. 'Last one up's a rotten zombie!'

And off he shoots.

For a few seconds I shake my head and tut loudly. Then, with a whoop, I leap, grab hold of a bar, pull myself up, steady myself on the rim and off I tear.

EIGHT

This is crazy. I know that even before I start. But hell, there's no denying it's fun! I haven't had an adrenalin rush like this since I returned to consciousness. Well, OK, it's not an actual adrenalin rush, since I doubt my body produces that any more. But it damn sure feels like it.

The rim of the wheel is thicker than I expected. A cable runs along the inside, good for gripping, but on the outside it's pure steel which isn't so accommodating.

At first it's easy. I scuttle along, no problem with my toughened flesh and bones. I laugh with delight, not bothered by the sunlight or what might happen to me if I fall, the gloom of the last week forgotten, focusing on nothing except my ascent.

Then it starts to get tricky. The higher I climb, the more gravity drags at me. From the ground the incline didn't look too steep, but when you're up here and following it, you get a fresh perspective. From about the quarter mark it's like climbing at ninety degrees. I start to slip and sway in the breeze, which seems much stronger than it did a few minutes ago.

I struggle on, teeth gritted, refusing to look at the ground. Cuts open on both hands as the steel and cable slice into them when I slip. Thankfully my blood doesn't flow as swiftly as it once did – it just seeps out slowly – or I'd have to stop. As it is, I can push on, pausing every so often to wipe the congealed blood from my palms.

I'm almost halfway up the wheel when I lose my grip completely. I fall with a cry that's cut short when I slam into one of the support poles which connects with the central bar. I cling on desperately as my legs swing freely beneath me. I hear Rage whooping with glee — he must have paused at the perfect time to catch my big slip. I'd love to shoot him the finger but I don't dare loosen my grip.

If I was human, I'd be done for. The wind would have been knocked from my sails, my muscles would be aching from the climb. Not being a Hollywood movie star, I doubt I'd be able to pull myself to safety. It would be the long drop for me.

But being dead has its advantages. I don't breathe, and my body isn't as confined by the laws of physics as it used to be. After dangling for a while, I haul myself up until I'm hanging across the bar. I wipe my hands dry, steady myself, grip the rim and start climbing again.

I'm just past the halfway mark when Rage shouts to me. 'Oi! Smith!' His voice is tinny, coming from so far away, but the wind carries it and my super-sharp ears pick it up.

I take a firm hold and look across to where he's hanging opposite me. My eyes are less effective than my ears, so he's only a vague blob in the distance. 'What?' I roar.

'What are we gonna do now?' he yells. 'It would be easier if we shifted to the outside of the rim. If we stick to the inside, we'll be hanging upside down the rest of the way.'

I'd been thinking about that myself. I was going to suggest we move to the other side, so we could crawl on top of the rim instead of dangle from its underside. But now that he's getting cold feet, I don't want to ease up. He was the dope who suggested this crazy challenge. I want to make him go through with it, even though that means me suffering as well.

'If you want to back down, let me know,' I roar cheerfully. 'I won't tell anyone you chickened out. Well, except for everyone we know.'

'Screw you!' he bellows. 'I'm game if you are.'

'Then what are you waiting for?' I laugh and start climbing again.

It soon becomes clear that we really *are* mad to attempt this. As hard as it was before, it's ten times more difficult now. I'm hanging from the rim like a squirrel, but squirrels have tails, padded paws and the benefit of countless generations of instinct to draw upon. Humans were never meant to climb like this, not even undead buggers like me.

The hardest parts are where the bars to the inner circle connect. The rim bulges out in those spots and I have to ease around the protuberances. That was easy on the lower sections, but not when I'm hanging upside down and every muscle in my arms is stretched to snapping point.

I keep my feet hooked over the rim for as much of the climb as I can, dragging them along, feeling the steel and cable slice deeply into my flesh. Pain doesn't hit you as much as it used to when you're a zombie, but we're not immune to it and I'm starting to really sting. I haven't felt this rough since I staggered away from Trafalgar Square after my last encounter with Mr Dowling.

My feet keep slipping. Eventually, when I move into the last quarter of the climb, I unhook them and hang at full stretch, supported solely by my hands. I was good on the monkey bars in playgrounds when I was a kid. I could swing across as often as I pleased, laughing at the others who couldn't match me. Time to find out if I still have the old magic.

I inch forward, moving my hands one at a time, concentrating as I never have before. I don't want to slip, and it's got nothing to do with the threat of smashing my skull open or the possibility that Rage will beat me to the top. I need to prove to myself that I can do this. As ludicrous as it is, this has become important to me. I figure if I can do this, I can attempt just about anything. Maybe this is what I need to clear my head and haul me out of the miserable, indecisive pit that I've been rotting in this past week.

It feels like the climb is never going to end. I want to shut my eyes but I can't. I want to take the strain from my arms but I can't. I want to rest for a while but ... You get the picture.

I spy Rage across from me. He hasn't made it as far as I have. He's struggling. He's stronger than me but a hell of a lot heavier too. In a situation like this, where weight comes into play, it's good to be a slim snip of a girl.

I get a second wind (relatively speaking) when I see that I'm doing better than Rage. With something between a triumphant shout and a despondent groan, I force myself on, finding fresh strength somewhere deep inside me, ignoring the pain, physics, gravity, the whole damn lot.

Finally, when I'm sure I can't go any further, I reach the highest point. I hang there for several long seconds, staring down at my feet and the drop beneath. I feel strangely peaceful. The pain in my arms seems to fade. If I fell right now and split my head open on a spoke, I could go happy into the great beyond.

But this isn't a day for bidding my final farewell to the

world. With a determined moan, I pull myself up, hook a leg over the rim, pause to let my arms recover, then search for the handles on the uppermost pod. Finding them, I haul myself up, almost scurrying compared to the slow pace of my previous progress, and moments later, I'm lying on top of the pod, staring at the clouds in the sky, a BIG smile on my face, waiting for the slow, shamed Rage to join me.

Bloody *yes*, mate!

NINE

Rage crawls on to the roof of the pod about a minute later. He's not huffing or puffing – with our redundant lungs we don't do that any more – but his limbs are shaking, especially his arms, the same way mine are.

'Sod me!' he gasps, collapsing on to his back and covering his eyes with a weary, trembling arm.

'No thanks,' I smirk, then dig him in the ribs with my knuckles. 'Who's the queen of the castle and who's a dirty rascal?'

'Get stuffed,' he barks.

'Come on, you set the challenge. Don't be a sore loser, just tell me who's the queen and –'

'Enough already,' he growls. 'You beat me fair and square. Happy?'

'Ecstatic,' I beam.

'I don't know how I made it,' Rage mutters. 'Those last

few metres were hell. I just wanted to drop and end the agony.'

'You're too big for climbing,' I chuckle. 'Size matters but sometimes it's better to be small.'

'Yeah,' he says. 'I guess.'

We lie there a while longer, relaxing, ignoring the glare of the daylight and the itching it causes. Then the Eye starts slowly revolving again. Ivor either saw us make the top or else he decided enough was enough.

I get to my feet to have a good look around. It's hard to see clearly without sunglasses to protect my eyes, but I force myself to turn and peer. Everything's blurred to begin with, but things start to swim into focus (well, as much as they're ever going to) as my eyes slowly adjust.

Rage stands up beside me. He doesn't bother with the sights, just rolls his arms around, working out the kinks and stretching his muscles.

'I bet we'll ache like hell later,' I note. 'We might even have to go back into the Groove Tubes.'

'Dr Oystein won't let us,' Rage says. 'He'll make us endure the pain. The Groove Tubes are for Angels who really need them, who get injured in the line of duty, not for thrill-seekers like us.'

'Oh well,' I smile, 'I don't care. It was worth it. I never thought I could have done something this amazing. You're still a murderous git, but you made a good call.'

'That's what I'm all about,' Rage says smugly. 'Making good calls and helping people realise their ambitions. The Good Samaritan had nothing on me.'

'He was bit more modest though.'

'Screw modesty,' Rage sniffs, then takes a step closer to me. 'Now, speaking of making good calls, here's another. B?'

I was looking off in the direction of Vauxhall, trying to see if there were any signs of life over there. When Rage calls my name, I turn to face him. My back's to the river.

'Enjoy your flight,' Rage says.

And he pushes me off.

My arms flail. I open my mouth to scream. Gravity grabs hold. I fall from the pod and plummet towards the river like a stone.

TEN

I hit the water hard. It feels like slamming into concrete. The lights temporarily blink out inside my head and everything goes dark.

When consciousness flickers on again, I think for a few seconds that I'm properly dead, adrift in a realm of ghosts. There are sinuous shadows all around, encircling and breaking over me. I assume that my brain was terminally damaged in the fall. I turn slowly, at peace, glad in a way to be done with life and all semblance of it. I spot a glimmering zone overhead — the legendary ball of light which summons the spirits of the departed?

No, of course not. After a brief moment of awe, I realise the truth. I'm still in the land of the living and the living dead. The shadows are nothing more than the eddies in the water. And the light is coming from the sun shining on the Thames.

I howl mutely, water rushing down my throat, cursing Rage and this world which refuses to relinquish its hold on me. Then, with disgust, I kick for the surface.

I haven't drifted far from the London Eye. I can still see it gleaming above me, turning smoothly. No sign of Rage but I hurl a watery insult his way regardless. Then I swim towards the bank and pull myself ashore close to a bridge. I lie on the pebbly, rubbish-strewn bank, next to the remains of a bloated corpse, and make myself throw up. Then I get to my legs – understandably shaky – and stagger to a set of steps, then up to the South Bank.

I slump to the ground in front of what used to be the Royal Festival Hall. There are some restaurants and shops at this level, all closed for business now. There's also an open, ramped section where teenagers used to practise on their rollerblades and skateboards. To my surprise and bewilderment, judging by the rumble of small, hard wheels, people are still using it.

I look up, wondering where the teenagers have come from, and how they dare take to the outdoors like this, when the area must be riddled with zombies. Then I realise they have nothing to fear from the zombies because they're undead too.

There are at least five or six of them, maybe a few more. They have the blank expressions common to all reviveds, but some spark of instinct is urging them to act as they did when they were alive, and they trundle around the gloomy space on their skateboards, rolling down ramps, grinding along bars, slamming into the graffiti-covered walls.

The skateboarding zombies are nowhere near as graceful as they must have been in life. They fall often, clumsily, their hands and faces covered in scars, and they don't try any sophisticated jumps or moves. But it's still a strangely uplifting sight, and I start to clap stiffly, feeling somebody should applaud their efforts.

When they hear me clapping, the zombies instantly lose interest in their boards. The teenagers growl with hungry excitement and dart towards me, flexing their fingers, sniffing the air, thinking supper has come early.

They can't see the hole in my chest, and I'm too tired to push myself upright, so I wave a weary hand in the air and they spot the bones sticking out of my fingertips. With some disappointed grunting sounds, they return to their patch, pick up the skateboards and start listlessly rolling around again, killing time until it's night and they can set out in search of brains.

I watch the show for a few minutes, then make myself puke again and more water comes up. For once I'm glad I don't have functioning taste buds — the water of the Thames was never the most inviting, but it's worse than ever these days, stained with the juices and rotting remains of the bodies you often see bobbing along.

I'm still trembling with shock. My head is throbbing. I think several of my ribs are broken. My left eyelid is almost fully shut now and won't respond to my commands. The fingers of both hands began to shake wildly when I stopped clapping and are spasming out of control.

I want to find Rage and rip his throat open, but in my sorry state I can't go anywhere at the moment. I just have to sit here, suffer pitifully and hope that I recover.

After a while, the clouds part. The sunlight stings my flesh and hurts my eyes, but helps dry me off. The warmth revives me slightly and the shakes begin to subside. When my hands are my own again, I roll on to my front, groaning, wishing the fall had put me out of my misery. I lie on the pavement like a dead fish, steam rising from my clothes, feeling sorry for myself, plotting my revenge on Rage.

A shadow falls across me. I look up through my right eye and spot a familiar face. Speak of the Devil . . .

'Have you clocked that lot?' Rage mutters, staring at the skateboarding teenagers.

'You're dead,' I gurgle.

'Aren't we all?' he laughs, squatting beside me. 'I half-hoped the fall would knock your brains out.'

'Only half?' I wheeze.

'Yeah. Despite what you think, I don't enjoy killing. I do it when necessary and don't worry about it, but I never wanted to become a serial killer. I'm not out to break any records on that front.'

'So why did you push me off?' I snarl, sitting up and shaking my head to get rid of the water in my ears.

'Making a point,' he says. 'I got sick of watching you mope around. Decided you needed a good, hard kick up the arse.' Rage stands and starts rolling his arms again, still aching from the climb. 'Dr Oystein would have done all he could to save you up there. If I'd told him what I was planning, he would have thrown himself between us and stood up for you. He's not like me. He doesn't think you're worthless scum.'

'That's your opinion of me?' I bristle.

Rage shrugs. 'It's my opinion of us all. I never thought people were anything special. A grim, brutal, boring lot. You got the occasional interesting person, like those skateboarders over there — still cool, even in death. But most of us were only good for breeding, fighting and screwing up the planet.'

'You're some piece of work,' I snort.

'Just being honest,' he smiles. 'I'm a lot of bad things but I'm not a hypocrite. I always saw people for what they were, and I never thought that was very much. Dr Oystein, on the other hand, sees the good stuff where I see the bad. He wants to make heroes out of me, you, Ivor and all the rest. I don't think he's gonna get very far with that, but I respect the mad old bugger for trying.'

'I'm sure he'd be delighted to hear that,' I sneer, getting up to face Rage.

'You need to accept the doc for what he is, or get the hell out of here,' Rage says softly. 'What I liked about you when we first met was that you stood up for your beliefs. You didn't like the way we were experimenting on the reviveds, so you refused to play ball. If you really don't trust Dr Oystein, you need to do that again. I hate seeing you mope around. You're better than that. Stronger than that.'

I stare at Rage, confused. He sounds like he's genuinely trying to help me. Or maybe he just wants me out of the way because I can see through him, because I know he's a threat.

'Listen up,' Rage says. 'These are your options. You can come back with me to County Hall, quit moaning and be a good little Angel like the rest of us. Or you can bugger off and look for a home elsewhere. Choose.'

'Screw you!' I roar, finding my fiery temper again. 'I don't have to do what you tell me!'

Rage grins. 'Are you gonna tell me I'm not the boss of you?'

I laugh despite myself. 'Bastard,' I mutter, shaking my head.

'B,' Rage says calmly, 'I'm saying all this because I think of you as an equal. I wouldn't bother with most of the others. They're mindless sheep, like the zom heads were. You need to get with the programme or get lost. If you're not happy here, go look for happiness somewhere else. You know the set-up with Dr Oystein. If you can't buy into it, get out now before you drive yourself mental.'

'And go where?' I mumble. 'Who'll look out for me apart from the doc and Mr Burke?'

'That doesn't matter,' Rage says. 'You're not a child, so don't act like one.'

'I'm more of a child than an adult,' I argue.

'Nah,' he says. 'We've all had to grow up since we died. You can look after yourself. You survived on your own before you came to County Hall. You can survive on your own again.'

'But I don't want to,' I whisper.

'Tough. You're acting like a sulky little girl. Nobody else will tell you to your face. I don't know if they're being diplomatic or if they're afraid of losing you, given how few of us there are. But you're not doing anyone any good like this. Be honest with me — does part of you wish you'd cracked your head open when I pushed you off the Eye? Were you tempted to not crawl out of the river, to just let it wash you away and dump you somewhere nobody could ever find you?'

I nod slowly, hating him for knowing me so well, hating myself for it being true.

'It's a big world,' Rage says. 'I'm sure there's a place in it, even for a moody cow like you.'

He turns to leave.

'Will you tell the others I said goodbye?' I call after him.

'No,' he grunts without looking back.

I treat myself to a grim smirk. Then, accepting the decision which Rage has helped me make, I push to my feet and cast one last longing glance in the direction of the London Eye and County Hall. Snorting water from my nose, I turn my back on them both and head off into the wilderness, abandoning the promise of friendship and redemption, becoming just another of the city's many lost, lonely, godforsaken souls.

ELEVEN

I limp along like a sodden rat, making my way past Waterloo before turning on to the Cut, once home to theatres, pubs and restaurants, now home only to the legions of the damned.

I don't look up much, just trudge along, head low, spirits even lower, cursing myself for being such a fool. Am I really going to turn my back on Dr Oystein, the Angels, Mr Burke and maybe the only sanctuary in the city that would ever accept someone like me? Can I really be that dumb?

Looks like it.

I make slow progress, hampered by my injuries and lack of direction. With nowhere to aim for, there's no need to rush. I'm itching like mad from the daylight but that doesn't deter me. I figure it's no more than a loser like me deserves. I don't even stop to pick up a pair of sunglasses or a hat.

I only pause when I reach Borough High Street. Borough

Market is just up the road. That was one of London's most famous food markets. Mum dragged me round it once, to check it out. She decided it wasn't any better than our local markets, and a lot more expensive, so she never came back.

I'm sure the food stocks have long since rotted, and even if they haven't, food is of no interest to me these days. But most of Borough Market was a dark, dingy place, built beneath railway viaducts. I bet the area is packed with zombies.

Ever since I revitalised, I've looked for a home among the conscious. Maybe that's where I've gone wrong. I might fit in better with the spaced-out walking dead.

I turn left and shuffle along. As I guessed, the old market is thronged with zombies, resting up to avoid the irritating light of the day world. I nudge in among them, drawing sharp, hungry stares. I rip a hole in the front of my T-shirt to expose the gaping cavity where my heart used to be. When they realise I'm one of their own, they leave me be.

All of the shops are occupied but I find a vacant spot in a street stall. There are a few rips in its canvas roof, through which old rainwater drips, but it's dry and shaded enough for me. There are even some sacks nearby which I shake out and fashion into a rough bed.

When I'm as comfortable as I can get, I take off my clothes and toss them away. No point leaving them out to dry — I can easily pick up replacements later. It doesn't matter to me that I'm lying here naked. The zombies aren't watching and there's nobody else around. Hell, maybe I won't bother with clothes again. I don't really need them in my current state, except to protect me from the sun when I go out in the daytime. But if I stick to the night world as my new comrades do ...

Dusk falls and the zombies stir. I head out with them to explore the city, interested to see where they go, how much ground they cover. I hunted with reviveds when I first left the shelter of the underground complex, but I never spent a huge amount of time in their company. I'd follow a pack until we found brains or, if they didn't seem to know what they were doing, I abandoned them and searched for another group.

Some of the zombies peel off on their own, but most stay in packs, usually no more than seven or eight per cluster. Hard to tell if they're grouped randomly or if these are old friends or family members, united in death as they were in life. They don't take much notice of one another – no hugging or fond looks – unless they communicate in ways that I'm not able to understand.

There's a woman in a wheelchair in one of the packs. Curious to see how she fares, I pick that one and stick with it for the whole night, trailing them round the streets of Borough and the surrounding area.

The zombie in the wheelchair has no problem keeping

up with the others. Like the skateboarding teenagers, she remembers on some deep, subconscious level how she operated when alive.

They don't seem to be moving in any specific direction though, taking corners without pausing to think, circling back on themselves without realising it, covering the same ground again. Their heads are constantly twitching as they stare into the shadows, sniff the air and listen for shuffling sounds which might signify life.

Rats are all over the place, foraging for food. They clearly don't consider the zombies much of a threat. And from what I see, they're right not to. One member of the pack catches a couple of rodents which were rooting around inside the carcass of a dog. He bites the head off each and chews them with relish. But those are the only successes of the night. The other zombies spend a lot of time stumbling after rats – the disabled woman launches herself from her wheelchair when she senses a kill, then sullenly drags herself back into it afterwards – but the fanged little beasts are too swift for them.

I know from chatting with the Angels that some zombies hole up in a particular place and stay there. Jakob did that when he was a revived, made his base in the crypt of St Martin-in-the-Fields. But these guys don't have that inclination, and rather than head back to the market when dawn breaks, they nudge into a house just off the New Kent Road and make a nest for the day.

The disabled woman struggles to mount the step into the house. She moans softly but the others don't help her. Finally she throws herself forward, leaving the chair to rest outside until she re-emerges when it's night again.

I stand by the wheelchair, scratching my head and scowling. I'd hoped to make a connection with the zombies of Borough Market, slot in with them, find a place to call my own. As deranged as they are, many still function as they did in the past, driven by instinct and habit to behave as they did when they were alive. I thought the locals of the market might grow used to me, nod at me when they saw me, invite me to hunt and eat with them.

Doesn't look like that's the case, not if this pack is anything to go by. They hunt together for some unknown reason, but they have no real sense of kinship. It's every zombie for him or herself.

I could go back and try again, follow another group when night falls and see if they prove any brighter or more welcoming. But what's the point? I'm not the same as these poor, lost souls, and there's nothing to be gained by pretending that I am. Why the hell would they bother about an outsider like me when they don't even truly care about their own?

'You're a mug, B,' I mutter. 'And getting muggier every day.'

With a sigh, I turn my back on the house of zombies and

head off on my own again. If a home exists for me in this city, it isn't among the reviveds. Not unless I choose to go without brains for a week or two. I'd revert if I didn't eat, lose my mind, become one of them.

It doesn't sound like much of an option, but I consider it seriously as I hobble away. After all, what's worse, having company as a brain-dead savage, or remaining in control of your senses but feeling lonely as hell all the time?

TWELVE

I can't tolerate the daylight without clothes. My skin itches like mad and my eyes feel as if they're being burnt from the inside out. So I make for the shopping centre in the Elephant and Castle. It's hardly a shopping mecca, but I find jeans, a T-shirt, a hoodie, a baseball cap and a jacket with a high collar. I pull on gloves and a few pairs of socks, finish up by tracking down some sunglasses.

I pick up a bottle of eye drops in a chemist's, and squirt in some of the contents while there. My eyes would dry out without regular treatment. I wouldn't go blind, but my vision would worsen.

I'm also going to need heavy-duty files for my fast-growing teeth and bones, since I left all mine at County Hall, but I can sort those out later. It will be a few days before my teeth start to bother me. Hell, maybe I'll just let the buggers grow. I mean, if I don't have anyone to chat with, what difference does it make?

Kitted out, and having ripped a hole in the front of the hoodie and T-shirt to reveal my chest cavity, I head back up the New Kent Road. I'm still in a lot of pain from the fall off the Eye, but I can cope with it as long as I don't rush. I've dealt with worse in the not too distant past.

I come to a roundabout and swing left on to Tower Bridge Road. I take my time, checking out the windows of old shops, acting like a tourist. I pause sadly when I come to Manze's, an old-style pie and mash shop, where they soak the pies and mashed potatoes in a sickly green sauce known as liquor. I wasn't into that sort of grub, but Dad loved it and he often talked about this place. He worked here for a while when he was a teenager. The stories he told were almost enough to turn me vegetarian. But as much as he'd spin wild tales about what went into the pies and liquor, he always swore this was the best pie and mash shop in London.

They used to do jellied eels too, and that reminds me of a guy I haven't thought about since finding my way to County Hall. Pursing my lips, I nod and carry on, a girl with a purpose, having made up my mind to go in pursuit of an actual target rather than just wander aimlessly.

As I'm coming to the junction of Tower Bridge Road and Tooley Street, I draw to a surprised halt and do a double take. Then I remove my sunglasses, just to be absolutely sure.

There's a sheepdog in the middle of the road.

The dog is lying down, clear of all the buildings, keeping a careful watch on the area around it, though it must be hard with all that hair over its eyes. It has a beautiful white chest, running to grey further back. Its hair is encrusted with dirt and old bloodstains. It pants softly and its tail swishes gently behind it.

I watch the dog for several minutes without moving. Finally, as if hypnotised, I start forward again, taking slow, cautious steps. The dog spots me and growls, getting to its feet immediately.

'It's all right,' I murmur. 'I'm not gonna hurt you. You're gorgeous. How have you survived this long? Are you lonely like me? I'm sure you are.'

The dog scrapes the road with its claws and growls again, but doesn't bark. It must have figured out that barking attracts unwanted attention. Zombies don't like the daylight, but they'll come out if tempted. There aren't many large animals left in this city — most of them were long ago hunted down and torn apart by brain-hungry reviveds. This dog knows that it has to be silent if it wants to survive.

I stop a safe distance from the dog and smile at it. I want it to trust me and come to me. I picture the pair of us

86

teaming up, keeping each other company, me looking out for the dog and protecting it from zombies, while in return it helps me find fresh brains. This could be the start of a beautiful friendship.

'You and me aren't that different,' I tell the dog. 'Survivors in a place where we aren't wanted. Alone, wary, weary. You should have headed out to the countryside. You'd be safer there. The pickings might be richer here but the dangers are much greater. Why haven't you left?'

The dog stares at me with an indecipherable expression. I don't know if it sees me as a threat or a possible mistress. Hell, maybe it sees me as lunch! I doubt a dog like this could be much of a threat, but maybe it's tougher than it looks. It might have survived by preying on zombies, ripping their throats open, using the element of surprise to attack and bring them down.

I spread my arms and chuckle at the thought of being taken out by a sheepdog. 'I'm all yours if you want me. I've no idea what zombies taste like, but anything must be better than rat.'

The dog shakes its head. I know it's just coincidence, that it can't understand what I'm saying, but I laugh with delight anyway.

'Stay here,' I tell it. 'I'll fetch a bone for you to chew and a ball to play with.'

I start to turn, to go and search the shops of Tower

Bridge Road. As soon as I move, the dog takes off, tearing down the street to my right, headed east.

'Wait!' I yell after it. 'Don't go. I won't hurt you. Come back. Please ...'

But the dog isn't listening. I don't blame it. I wouldn't trust a zombie either, even one who can speak. It won't have lasted this long by taking chances. A creature in that position will have learnt to treat every possible threat as a very real challenge to its existence. Better to run and live than gamble and die.

I stay where I am for a while, reliving my encounter with the dog, smiling at the memory, hoping it will come back to sniff me out if I don't move. But in the end I have to accept that the dog has gone. I stare one last time at the spot where it was lying, then push on over the bridge, alone but not quite as lonely as I felt a few minutes before.

THIRTEEN

I glance at HMS *Belfast* as I'm crossing the bridge, remembering the last time I wandered past. There were people on-board then, heavily armed, and they opened fire as soon as they saw me. I'm too far away to see if they're still there, but I've no wish to go check. Hostile hotheads with guns are best left to their own devices.

As I draw close to the Tower of London, I recall the Beefeater who tackled me when I tried to sneak past. I wonder if he's still guarding the entrance, demanding a ticket from anyone who wants to enter. I bet he is. In an odd way I feel sorry for him. I'd like to take him some brains, a little surprise gift. I examine the corpses littered across the bridge, but their skulls have been scraped clean. Oh well, maybe another time.

I slowly make my way towards Whitechapel, then up Brick Lane. It feels like years since I was last here, even though it can't be more than ... what? Two months or so, and I spent a good deal of that in the Groove Tube. I blame my skewed perception on not being able to sleep. Time moves much more sluggishly when you can't drop off at night.

I come to the Old Truman Brewery. The steel door is locked and there's no sign of life inside. But then there wouldn't be. Its artist-in-residence might be a God-obsessed nutter like Dr Oystein, but he's smart enough to keep a low profile when at home. If he was in – which he probably isn't, since the sun's been up for quite a while and he's an early starter – I wouldn't know it from out here.

I don't knock on the door or bellow the artist's name. I could attract company if I did. Instead I lower myself to the ground, sit by the door and wait, patient as a spider. It might be a waste of time – a zombie might have snagged him ages ago – but I've nothing better to be doing.

The day passes slowly. I miss Master Zhang – time flew by when I was training with him – and the Angels. Even a sneering match with Rage was preferable to sitting on my own on a deserted street all day.

I don't see any other living or undead creatures, except for some rats who give me a wide berth. And insects of course. Lots and lots of insects. The streets are awash with them. Zombies have no interest in ant or cockroach brains, so they don't hunt them. They're not creeped out by insects either – it takes a lot to startle a walking corpse – so they don't bother stamping on them or doing anything else to keep them in check.

I pass the hours counting the different types of insects that I see. I lose track a few times, until eventually I give up altogether. Then, late in the afternoon, I spot a man walking along, lugging an easel and whistling softly. I bet he doesn't know that he's whistling. He must be doing it subconsciously, unaware of the noise he's making. Even a soft whistle like that could bring a pack of zombies down on him, daylight or not.

He's almost at the door before he spots me. As soon as he does, he yelps, drops the easel and turns to flee.

'It's all right, Timothy,' I call. 'It's me, B.'

He pauses and looks back uncertainly. 'Mee-bee?'

'No, you dope.' I stand, groaning as fresh pain flares in my battered bones. 'It's me — B. Becky Smith. Remember?'

Timothy's expression clears. 'Of course. B Smith, the talking zombie. I'm so delighted that you're still going strong. How are you? What have you been up to?'

Timothy bounds forward, smiling widely, hand outstretched. He's wearing the same sort of clothes as before, yellow trousers, a purple shirt, a tweed jacket. His brown hair is even longer than when I last saw him, shot through with streaks of paint. His eyes are still swamped by terribly dark circles in his long, thin face.

'You don't want to shake hands with me,' I tut. 'I'm not safe.'

He comes to an immediate stop. 'Oh, that's right. I was so excited to see you, I forgot. Silly me.' He lowers his hand and chuckles. 'As you can probably tell, I haven't spoken to anyone since we last met. I'm desperate for company. The painting keeps me going, but there's nothing like a good old bit of gossip to really stir the senses.'

Timothy retrieves his easel and checks to make sure it hasn't been broken.

'I had hoped to see you sooner than this,' he says, trying to phrase it lightly. 'I thought you might come and visit me. When you didn't, I assumed you had either been welcomed with open arms by the soldiers you went off in pursuit of, or had been mown down by them.'

'The latter,' I grimace. 'They opened fire when they realised I was undead, even shot a missile at me from a helicopter.'

'But you survived and escaped?' Timothy claps enthusiastically. 'Top-drawer! Where have you been since then? Why didn't you come back? I've painted some marvellous images. I'd love to share them with you.'

'I've been busy,' I mutter. 'Things took a strange turn. Have you been over to County Hall since you started painting?'

'A few times,' he nods. 'I sketched it from the north bank of the river.'

'You should wander south. You'd find a whole lot of interesting stuff to paint.'

'That sounds intriguing,' he purrs. 'I look forward to hearing all about it. You are staying, aren't you? For a while at least?'

'If I'm welcome, yeah.'

'Of course you're welcome,' Timothy booms, bouncing to the door and getting out his key. 'And you aren't the only one with news to share. I've played host to a most unique visitor since our paths last crossed. I'll have to introduce you, see what your opinion is, if you can make any more sense of it than I have.'

I squint at him. 'I thought you said you hadn't been talking to anyone since I left you.'

'I haven't,' he smirks. 'This guest isn't much of a one for talking. But I think you'll be fascinated nevertheless. And who knows, maybe you'll manage to draw a response of some sort. I believe you might have more in common with the strange little dear than I have.'

He laughs at my confused expression, then throws open the door and ushers me inside, politely asking me to wipe my feet on the way.

FOURTEEN

Timothy Jackson is an artist who survived the zombie attacks. Rather than lie low afterwards or flee the city as so many others did, he decided to make paintings of the downfall of London. Like Dr Oystein, he thinks he has been hand-picked by God, except in his case the Almighty only wants him to record images of the mayhem, not put a stop to it.

Once Timothy has stowed his equipment, he leads me upstairs, through a room of mostly blank canvases, to one crowded with finished works. It's even more jam-packed than it was the last time I was here. There's barely space to move.

'You've been busy,' I note.

'Yes,' he says with passion. 'I feel like I've really hit my stride these last few weeks. I'm getting faster, without having to compromise my style. Here, look at this.'

He shows me a large painting of a mound of bodies stacked in a heap, St Paul's Cathedral rising behind them in the distance. Many of the faces are vague blobs and splashes of paint, but he's paid close attention to detail on a few of them, and also to the cathedral.

'Two days to complete,' he says proudly. 'That would have been at least a week's work just a couple of months ago, and I doubt I could have captured the expressions as clearly as I did. I'm improving all the time. Another year and who knows what I might be capable of.'

'How did the bodies end up in a pile like that?' I ask, staring at the morbid painting. 'Did you gather them together?'

'Certainly not,' Timothy huffs. 'I paint only what I find. I never stage a scene. That would be cheating.'

'Then how . . . ?' I ask again.

'They were zombies,' Timothy says softly. 'They'd been shot, I assume by soldiers or hunters. If by soldiers, I imagine they stacked the bodies that way in order to come back and incinerate them at some point in the future. If by hunters, I suppose they did it so that they could pose for photos in front of their kills.'

'Sometimes I think that your kind are worse than mine,' I growl, recalling my own brush with the American hunter, Barnes, and his posse. 'I've no problem with survivors killing zombies because of the threat we pose, but doing it for sport is sick.'

'I agree,' Timothy says. 'Humans are far more dangerous than the undead. I keep my head down when I hear gunfire. I know where I stand with zombies, but I never know what to expect from the living.'

Timothy heads for the larder, washing his hands along the way, and prepares a simple meal for himself, cold beans on bread, some tinned carrots and a glass of red wine to wash it all down.

'Why don't you heat the food?' I ask.

'Zombies might pick up the smell,' he explains. 'I avoid cooking when I can. On those days when I simply *must* have a hot meal, I set up a barbecue in a park or public square and cook a big lunch. I tried cooking in a restaurant's kitchen once and was almost caught. I only barely got out alive.'

Timothy has a mouthful of wine after he tosses away the tins, before tucking into his meagre meal. He closes his eyes dreamily, savouring the taste, then cocks an eyebrow at me. 'Are you sure you won't share a glass?'

'Apart from brains, I can't process anything,' I tell him. 'Liquids run clean through me. If I had any of that, I'd be sitting in a puddle by the end of the night.'

Timothy clears his throat. 'Ah. That might explain ... I don't wish to be rude, but you might want to ...' He wags a finger at me.

'What are you talking about?'

'When I was coming up the stairs behind you, I couldn't help but notice that the back of your trousers seemed rather damp.'

My right eyelid flies wide open. (The left lid still doesn't work properly.) I feel behind and, sure enough, my fingers come away soaking.

'Damn it! I fell into the Thames yesterday and swallowed a load of water. I puked up most of it but obviously not all. Sorry about this.'

'No need to apologise,' Timothy says. 'We all have our crosses to bear. Can I be of any assistance? There are plenty of towels and sheets here. If you wish, I could fashion you a . . .'

'. . . nappy?' I growl.

Timothy gulps and smiles sheepishly.

'Don't worry about it,' I chuckle. 'A wet bum is the least of my worries. I'll be happy with a towel to sit on, if that's all right with you.'

'Absolutely.' Timothy hurries off and comes back with two thick towels which he carefully places on a plastic chair. He waits for me to sit and give him the OK before taking his own seat and tucking into his food with a plastic knife and fork that he probably picked up in a take-away.

We chat as Timothy eats. He asks me where I went when I left him and I talk him through my trip to the West End, my run-in with Barnes and the other hunters, Sister Clare and her mad Order of the Shnax, their gruesome finale in Liverpool Street, all the rest. I hesitate when I get to the Trafalgar Square part of the story, finding it hard to talk about even now.

'The soldiers drove you away?' Timothy asks sympathetically.

'No. They tried to kill me. They would have too – they had me pegged – except for Mr Dowling and his mutants.'

I expect Timothy to look blank, but to my surprise he knows what I'm talking about. He was working on his last slice of bread, but now he lays it down and stares at me. 'You've seen the mutants?'

'Yeah.'

His voice drops. 'And the clown?'

'Oh yeah. That's Mr Dowling.'

'You know his name?' Timothy sounds amazed.

'Of course. There's a big badge on his chest with his name on it.'

'Really? I never got that close to him. And the man with the eyes? Do you know him too?'

I make a growling noise. 'Him especially. He paid me a home visit back before all the madness started. I call him Owl Man. You've seen him too?'

Timothy nods, then stands and scurries away from

the table, beckoning for me to follow. He leads me back to the room of finished canvases and roots through a pile stacked against one of the walls. I'd find it hard to distinguish between them since it's so dark – the windows are boarded over – but his eyes must have adjusted to the gloom over the months he's spent living and working here.

'I hung this up when I finished it,' he mumbles as he searches, 'but it gave me the shivers, so I took it down again. Those eyes followed me every time I passed, and not in a good way.'

He produces a medium-sized canvas and carries it to one of the rooms with no windows, the only places in the building where he dares turn on lights at night. He sets the painting down and stands back to study it, then slides aside to make space for me.

I don't recognise any of the buildings, just plain office blocks that could be anywhere in London. But there's no mistaking the horrific clown at the centre of the painting, Mr Dowling in all his dreadful finery. I'm familiar with the mutants surrounding him too, in their standard hoodies, with their rotting skin and yellow eyes.

And there's Owl Man, tall and thin, except for a ridiculously round pot belly. He has white hair and pale skin, but doesn't appear to be deformed in any other way. Except for his eyes, the largest I've ever seen, at least twice the size of mine. They're almost totally white, but with an incredibly dark, tiny pupil at the heart of each.

'If I hadn't seen him in the flesh, I wouldn't have believed his eyes could have been that big,' I whisper.

'I know,' Timothy says. 'I almost made them smaller, to make them appear more in keeping with the size of his face, but I try not to distort reality when I paint.'

'What were they doing?' I ask.

'Just talking. At least the man with the eyes was talking. The clown didn't seem to say much.'

'He can't speak. He communicates with his mutants by making squeaking noises which they can interpret.'

Timothy stares at me. 'You seem to know a lot about them.'

'Our paths have crossed a few times.'

I study Mr Dowling and Owl Man. The clown is the more frightening of the two, but Owl Man's eyes are unsettling — as Timothy said, they seem to follow me when I move. I wouldn't want to run into either of those eerie men on a dark night. Or a sunny day, come to that.

'Where did you see them?' I ask, turning away from the painting and trying to put it from my thoughts.

'Somewhere in the City,' Timothy says. 'I was wandering as normal, saw them in the distance and decided after one look that they weren't the sort of people I'd like to get better acquainted with. I managed to sneak close enough to sketch them. They didn't hang around for very long. As soon as they left, I hurried back here and worked up the painting. I didn't want to forget any of the finer details.'

'When was this?'

He has to think. 'Not long after you left. Maybe a week or so after.'

'Have you seen them since?'

He shakes his head. 'I haven't been looking either. There are some things which even I shy away from. I'm determined to capture this city in all its nightmarish glory, but I've a feeling I wouldn't last long if that clown and his crew were aware of me. I doubt they'd be as easy to shake off as the zombies if they gave chase.'

'You've got that right,' I sigh. 'They let me go for some reason, but if they'd wanted to stop me, I don't think I could have done a hell of a lot about it.'

'Do you know anything else about them?' Timothy asks. 'Where they came from, what they are, what they might be planning?'

'No.' I chuckle sickly. 'But I know a man who does. At least he thinks he does. You're not the only guy working for God in London. And if this other prophet is to be believed, that clown is your direct opposite. If you were sent by God to paint the city as you find it, that nasty bugger was sent by the Devil to paint it black.'

Timothy gawps at me, lost for words. I laugh at his expression and shake my head. 'Come on, let's go back to the kitchen. I'll tell you all about it while you finish your food. Those creeps aren't worth missing a meal over.'

FIFTEEN

I tell Timothy about my weird encounters with Mr Dowling and his merry mutants, how we first met in the underground complex, and how he later spared my life in Trafalgar Square.

'I don't know why he didn't kill me. Although, having said that, I haven't seen him harm any zombies. Maybe he only kills living people.'

'That's a great comfort to me,' Timothy sniffs.

'Don't worry,' I grin. 'You must have the luck of the Devil to have survived this long and, according to Dr Oystein, Mr Dowling is the Devil's spawn, so you're both in the same boat. He'd probably look upon you as a long-lost cousin.'

'Why do you keep talking about the Devil?' Timothy frowns. 'And who is this doctor you've referred to?'

'I'm coming to it,' I tut. 'What's the rush? We've got all night.'

'You might have,' Timothy says, 'but I have to sleep, or had you forgotten?'

'Do you know,' I say softly, 'I had. It's been so long since I've slept that I've forgotten that it wasn't always this way, that there are people out there who don't have to sit up all night counting the circles on their fingers.'

'Those are called whorls,' Timothy informs me.

'Whorl my arse,' I snort, then tell Timothy what happened after the battle between the soldiers and Mr Dowling, finding the Angels in County Hall, training with them, Dr Oystein's revelation about God's plans for him.

Timothy's last piece of bread remains uneaten, the beans soaking into it until it's a soggy mess. He's too engrossed in my story to focus on food. He hardly even sips his wine.

'Incredible,' he murmurs when I finish. 'What a load to take upon oneself. To bear responsibility for the future of the world ... He has my admiration whether his story is true or not.'

'Of course it's not true,' I snap. 'He's a nutter like Sister Clare and ...'

I pause pointedly, waiting for Timothy to say wryly, '... and *me*?' But he only stares at me blankly. He's so sure of his calling that he finds it impossible to think that anyone might question him.

'Anyway,' I chuckle, not wanting to burst poor Timothy's bubble, 'I tried to overlook his God complex and fit in with the others, but in the end I couldn't stomach it, so I left.'

Timothy nods slowly, then stares into his glass of wine, swirling the liquid around. He purses his lips, looks at the bread and beans, then picks up the plate and takes it to the sink to clean.

'Do you think Dr Oystein is a liar or a madman?' Timothy asks while washing the plate in a bucket of cold water.

'Mad,' I reply instantly. 'He believes everything he says.'

'You don't think he is trying to con you?'

'No.'

Timothy stands the plate on a rack to dry, then turns and looks at me seriously.

'In that case, maybe he's right. Maybe he *is* a servant of God.'

'Nah.'

'How can you be so sure?' Timothy challenges me.

'Because . . .' I scowl. 'Look, I don't want to piss you off, but it's rubbish, isn't it? God, the Devil, Heaven and Hell, reincarnation. I mean, I dunno, maybe there's some truth to some of it, but nobody can be sure. There have been so many different religions over the years, so many *truths*. How can one be right and all the others wrong?'

'I don't think it's about being absolutely right,' Timothy says. 'The main message of most religions is the same — be kind to other people, lead an honourable life, don't cause trouble. I've always seen God as a massive diamond with thousands – maybe millions – of faces. We get a different view of the diamond, depending on which angle we look at it from. But there must be *something* there, otherwise what are we all looking at?'

'Maybe you're right,' I huff. 'I'm no expert, far from it. But there's more to why I left than the religious angle. It's the whole . . .' I grimace, not sure how to put my thoughts into words.

'Look,' I try, 'I've never seen ghosts, vampires or anything like that. This isn't a supernatural world. I believe in evolution. I'm sure there's life spread around the universe, more aliens out there than we can imagine. But I bet they're the same as us in that they just roll along wherever the universe pushes them, bound by the laws of nature as we are.'

'My mother swore that she often saw the ghosts of her parents,' Timothy murmurs. 'They died when she was a girl, yet she never missed them because she saw so much of them as she grew up.'

'Did she see fairies too?' I sneer.

'No,' Timothy says calmly. 'She was a mathematician. She had a doctorate from Cambridge. One of the sharpest minds in her field according to those who knew about such things. She wasn't especially religious. But she saw ghosts and accepted them as real. She even developed a mathematical equation to explain their relationship to the material world, though obviously I couldn't make head or tail of that.'

'All right,' I nod. 'Sorry for poking fun at her. But that kind of proves my point. You say she came up with a formula to describe how ghosts work. I can accept that. There are all sorts of weird things in the world, but they can be explained with maths and science. There's nothing miraculous about them.'

'I disagree,' Timothy says. 'This *is* a world of miracles, of things which defy explanation, maybe even understanding. You're proof of that, a reanimated corpse, a girl whose soul has been restored. You might not believe in ghosts or vampires, but surely you believe in zombies?'

'Very clever,' I growl as he smirks at me. 'But there's nothing God-inspired about us. We're the result of an experiment gone wrong. I wasn't created by God, just as Dr Oystein wasn't given heavenly orders to save the world from the Devil's henchman. This mess is our own fault, and if we're gonna fix it and put the world back together, we have to do it ourselves.'

Timothy thinks about that. He finishes his wine and pours another glass. Takes a long, pleasing sip.

'What if you're wrong?' he asks quietly.

'I'm not.'

'You can't be sure of that,' he presses. 'Using your own logic, no one can truly know the workings of the universe, or how much of a role God might play in our day-to-day lives. What if the creator *did* choose Dr Oystein? There's no way of proving it, it's purely a matter of faith. But surely we all have to put our faith in someone. If you choose not to believe this particular prophet, fine, maybe you're right to doubt him. But why are you so set against even the possibility that he might be telling the truth?'

'Because it would stink if it was true!' I shout, then swiftly lower my voice, not wanting to alert any zombies which might be passing by outside.

'According to Dr Oystein, God knew this was going to happen. He had decades of warning, and what did He do in all that time? Nothing, except give one guy the power to try and light the flames of a revival once the world had gone to hell. What sort of a God could do something like that to us?'

'A God who isn't the same as we are,' Timothy says. 'A God who has more to worry about than just our fate. A God who maybe has an eye on billions of worlds, who can't afford to spend His entire time trying to steer one particular species in the right direction. We can't understand the mind of God and, from what you say, Dr Oystein doesn't claim to. He's simply doing what was asked of him. I can buy into that, a God who doesn't govern directly, but who tries to lend a helping hand. In a way I'd prefer that to a God who ruled by divine decree.'

'The only person who lent Dr Oystein a helping hand is himself,' I jeer. 'The voice in his head is his own. It has to be.'

'It doesn't,' Timothy insists. 'This is a world of marvels and wonders. A world of miracles, if you wish to put it that way. In such a world, why can't God speak to Dr Oystein or anyone else?'

'Because it's *not* a world of marvels,' I snarl. 'It's a world of science, maths and nature.'

'*And* miracles,' Timothy says stubbornly. 'There are things which science can't explain, wonders which confirm there is more to this universe than we know.'

He downs the remains of his wine and sighs with contentment. Then he stands, a sparkle to his eyes.

'It's time I let you see my other visitor,' he says. 'Perhaps then you will be more inclined to accept the reality of the miraculous.'

'If it's not Elvis Presley or Michael Jackson, I'll be very disappointed,' I joke.

'It's neither of those fine men,' he says. 'But you'll be impressed regardless, I guarantee it.'

Then he leads me from the room and up the stairs of the echoing old brewery in search of wonder.

SIXTEEN

Timothy guides me to a small room just off the massive area where most of his paintings are stacked. I recall spotting this door the last time we came through. I thought it was a storage room or something like that. And maybe it was once. But not any longer. Now it's been turned into a bizarre nursery.

There's a cot in the middle of the room. Several mobiles hang from the ceiling. Lots of dolls and cuddly toys are stacked neatly in the corners. There's a large, inflatable dinosaur. Soft balls. A couple of activity gyms. A mix of blue and pink curtains draped around the walls.

'It's overkill, I know,' Timothy says with a sheepish chuckle. 'I just couldn't help myself. I had to have anything that I thought my guest might enjoy. It's not like there are limits any more. The shops are full of toys that will never be used. Why not spoil the poor creature? Although, having said that, I don't know if the little dear notices any of this.'

'What are you talking about?' I start towards the cot, then stop dead. 'Don't tell me it's a zombie baby. It is, isn't it? You've adopted a bloody undead baby!'

'B . . .' he starts to defend himself.

'What the hell were you thinking?' I shout. 'I don't care how cute it might look — if it's a zombie, it's deadly. One scratch or nip and you're history. I can't believe you'd risk everything just so you can play daddy.'

'It's not a zombie,' Timothy says without losing his temper.

I stare at the cot suspiciously. 'Are you telling me it's a real baby?'

'I wouldn't describe it that way either.'

'You're not making sense,' I scowl.

'That's why you have to go and look,' he smiles.

I don't want to. Something about this feels wrong. I want to back out and get far away from here and whatever's in the cot. But fascination propels me.

I edge forward cautiously, ready to turn and run if I sense a threat. Then I come within sight of the baby and I freeze. My right eye widens and even my injured left eyelid lifts a bit. I feel the walls of reality crumbling around me, the world tilting on its axis, the fingers of a nightmare reaching out to grab me.

The baby is dressed in a long, white christening gown. Its tiny hands are crossed on its chest. Its nails are sharper and more jagged than a normal baby's, but no bones jut out of the fingertips. Its feet are hidden by the folds of the gown.

Its face is a stiff mask, like a cross between a human's and a doll's, but there's nothing human about its mouth and eyes. The small mouth is open, full of tiny, sharp teeth. Its eyes are pure white balls, no pupils. Its eyelids don't flicker, though its lips twitch regularly and an occasional tremor runs through its cheeks.

A metal spike has been stuck through the baby's head. The spike enters the skull above the left eyebrow and the tip pokes out just behind the baby's left ear.

'Have you ever seen anything like that?' Timothy whispers.

'It's not real,' I croak.

'I thought that too at first,' he says. 'I was sure it was a doll or a zombie. But it has a heartbeat. And if you watch closely, you'll see its chest rise and fall — it's breathing, just very slowly.'

'It can't be real,' I whisper. Then I add numbly, in answer to his question, 'Yes. I've seen babies like that before.'

'Where?' Timothy frowns.

'In my dreams.'

I used to have a recurring nightmare when I was alive. I'd be on a plane and it would fill with babies that looked just like this one. In the dream they'd call me their mummy and clamber over me, ask me to join them, tear at me, bite, rip me apart, tell me I was one of them now.

That dream terrified me all of my life. I thought I'd finally escaped it when I stopped sleeping. But now it's somehow followed me out of the realm of the unreal and into the wide-awake world.

'You can't have dreamt of anything like this grisly beauty,' Timothy says, dismissing my claim with a wave of his hand. 'I took off its clothes when I brought it back. I wanted to see if it had been infected — I assumed it had to be a zombie, even with its heartbeat.

'It's not. No marks anywhere. No bites, scratches, nothing. Except for the spike through its head of course. I thought there might be undead germs on the metal, that the reason the child showed signs of life was because the zombie virus had first attacked its brain and then been inhibited by the position of the spike. And maybe there's something to that theory. But it doesn't explain . . .'

Timothy takes hold of the hem of the baby's gown and lifts it, exposing the child's feet, legs and more.

'Bloody hell!' I shout.

'. . . *this*,' Timothy exhales softly.

The baby doesn't have any genitals. There's nothing but smooth flesh between its thighs.

'It doesn't have an anus either,' Timothy says, and for

some reason that makes me laugh hysterically. Timothy blinks with surprise and adds, 'I can turn it over if you want to check.'

I stop laughing abruptly. Then I moan, 'Do me a favour and lower the gown. I've seen enough.'

Timothy lays the gown back in place and smooths down the hem.

'What is it?' I hiss.

'I don't know,' Timothy says. He waits a few beats, then grins wickedly. 'It's a *miracle*.'

'No,' I choke. 'There's nothing miraculous about a freak like that. Diabolical, maybe.'

'Don't say such things,' Timothy frowns. 'It's only a baby. It can't help the way it's been put together.'

'But who created it?' I ask, voice rising again. 'Where did it come from? How can it live with a spike through its head?'

'I don't know,' Timothy says, smiling lovingly at the white-eyed baby. 'But that's not the only remarkable thing. I found the child maybe three weeks ago. It was lying in the road close to the Aldgate East Tube entrance, near Whitechapel Art Gallery. That was one of my favourite galleries. Did you ever visit it?'

I shake my head, unable to glance away from the unnatural child.

'The baby hasn't eaten in all that time,' Timothy continues.

114

'I tried to feed it milk and biscuits when I first rescued it, but it wouldn't swallow. I was going to poke a tube down its mouth and force-feed it, but I decided there was no point keeping the poor creature alive in such a pitiable condition. So I sat back and left it to nature, waiting for it to die.

'As you can see, it hasn't. It's in the same condition today as it was when I found it.'

'But how?' I ask again. 'What is it? Where did it come from?'

'Like you, I've been asking those questions over and over,' Timothy says. 'No answers have presented themselves. For the first few days I didn't leave its side. I stood watch, waiting for it to die, putting my work on hold. When I saw that it wasn't going to pass away, I returned to my normal routine, though I spend most of my nights in here now. I've started reading stories to it. I don't know if it can hear me or understand what I'm saying, but I like reading out loud.'

Timothy looks around at everything that he's gathered and sighs. 'Like I said, I know it's overkill, but I can't stop bringing back presents. I guess I was lonelier than I realised.'

'Has it ever said anything?' I ask, moving closer to the baby, staring at its teeth – *fangs* – and pale white lips.

'No. Its mouth moves but always silently. What age do you think it is? When do babies start to speak?'

I can't answer those questions. I don't really care.

'The babies in my dreams could speak,' I whisper. 'I need to know if this one can, if it says the same sort of things that they used to.'

'How could it?' Timothy scoffs. 'This isn't from your dreams. It's real.'

'Still . . .' I reach towards the baby.

'What are you doing?' Timothy snaps.

'I'm going to pull out the spike.'

'Are you hell!' he shouts, pushing me away.

'Easy,' I say, putting my hands behind my back, wary of accidentally scratching and infecting him. 'I don't want to hurt it. But I have to find out.'

'You're not going anywhere near that spike,' Timothy growls. 'It holds the poor thing's brain in place. If you pull out the spike, you'll kill it.'

'I wouldn't be so sure of that,' I mutter. 'But even if I do, so what? Look at it, Timothy. That's no normal baby. Whatever it is, wherever it came from, it's not one of us. One of *you*,' I correct myself.

'Even so, it's alive and defenceless and I've sworn to protect it,' Timothy says grandly.

'The damn thing has a spike through its head,' I remind him. 'It's a bit too late for protection.'

'Spike or no spike, it's still alive,' Timothy argues.

'But what sort of a future does it have?' I press. 'For all we know it's in agony and is silently begging for someone to end its pain. Maybe it will recover if we remove the spike. Who knows how a thing like this might function? For all we know, it doesn't even have a brain.

'It has no quality of life,' I say, taking a step towards the cot. Timothy doesn't try to stop me this time. 'If we leave it as it is, it will definitely die in the end, whether it needs food or not. This way it has a chance. We might save it.'

'Do you really believe that?' Timothy whispers.

'Yeah,' I lie.

'I only want what's best for the little darling,' he sighs.

'This is the way forward,' I assure him. 'We can cover the hole with a bandage if we need to, maybe even stick the spike back in. It's risky, I won't deny it, but what choice do we have?'

'We could stand by and not interfere,' Timothy says, then shakes his head. 'No. You're right. That would be selfish of me. This way it has a chance. Go on, B. I'll support you. I won't blame you if it goes wrong.'

I stretch out a trembling hand and grip the spike above the baby's eye. I stare again at that pure white orb, remembering the babies in my dreams, how their eyes turned red when they attacked me. I gulp. Tighten my grip. And pull.

The spike comes out with very little resistance. There's a small sucking sound as it clears the clammy flesh. Blood oozes out of the hole, but slowly, not in huge amounts. A few bits of brain trickle from the spike.

Timothy and I stare at the baby. Neither of us says a word.

Nothing happens.

Then, maybe a full minute after I've withdrawn the spike from the baby's head, it shudders. Its arms uncross and its fingers claw at the blankets beneath it. As I watch with disbelief and horror, its eyes turn red, as if filling with blood, and it starts to scream in a terrifyingly familiar, tinny voice. '*mummy. mummy. mummy. mummeeeeeEEEEEEE.*'

SEVENTEEN

The baby keeps squealing, the same word repeated without even a pause for breath, calling for its *mummy*. The high-pitched noise cuts through me, making me wince and grind my teeth. Timothy is staring slack-jawed at the whining, red-eyed child.

'Make it stop,' I bark, covering my ears with my hands.

'How?' Timothy asks.

'Stick the spike back in its head.'

'No,' he says, face turning a shade paler at the thought. 'We can't do that. Let's find it a dummy.'

He lurches to a shelf stacked with baby stuff. He roots through the neat pile until he finds one. He hurries back and leans over the cot, cooing to the hellish baby, 'There, there. It's all right. We'll take care of you. No need to cry. Does it hurt? We'll make the pain go away. You're our little baby, aren't you?'

'Less of that crap,' I snort, shuddering at the thought of being mother to such an unearthly creature. 'Just shut the damn thing up.'

'Be nice, B,' Timothy tuts, then yelps and takes a quick step away from the cot. 'It tried to bite me!'

'Oh, give it to me,' I snap, nudging him aside and taking the dummy from him. I bend over, fingers of my left hand extended to widen the baby's mouth if necessary. Before I can touch its lips, the tiny creature's head shoots forward and its fangs snap shut on the bones sticking out of my middle and index fingers.

'Let go!' I roar with fright and try to pull my hand free. The baby rises with my arm, dangling from the bones, fangs locked into them, chewing furiously, head jerking left and right.

I wheel away from the cot, shaking my arm, trying to dislodge the monstrous infant. Timothy is yelling at me to be careful, not to drop the child. I swear loudly and try to hurl the baby loose.

I lose my balance, crash into the inflatable dinosaur and stumble to my knees. As I push myself to my feet again, the baby chews through the bones, drops to the floor and collapses on its back. It immediately resumes screaming for its mummy.

'Bloody hell!' I pant, retreating swiftly. My hand is trembling.

'I told you it wasn't a good idea,' Timothy says smugly. 'It obviously doesn't want a dummy, and with teeth like that, who are we to argue?'

'Sod what it wants,' I snarl. 'We have to shut it up.'

'You can try again if you wish,' Timothy chuckles. 'Personally I like my fingers the way they are. Those teeth are amazing. I wonder what they're made of?'

'You go on wondering,' I growl, crossing the room to pick up the spike. 'I'm putting a stop to this.'

'No,' Timothy says sternly. 'You can't do that.'

'I bloody well can,' I huff, advancing on the wailing baby. Timothy steps in my way and crosses his arms.

'Move it, painter-boy. I'm not playing games.'

'Neither am I,' he says. 'You're not sticking that into the baby's head. You might kill it.'

'Do I look like I care?'

'No. That's why I can't let you proceed. You're not thinking clearly. You're upset and alarmed, understandably so. But when you calm down, you'll see that I'm right. This is a living baby, calling for its mother. It's afraid and lonely, probably in pain and shock. We have to comfort it, not treat it like a rabid animal that needs to be exterminated.'

'Didn't you see what it did with those teeth?' I roar, waving my gnawed fingerbones at him.

'Yes, but to be fair, you were attacking it. I would have bitten in self-defence too if you'd come at me like that.'

'But you wouldn't have been able to chew through my bones,' I note angrily.

'So its teeth are tougher than ours,' he shrugs. 'What of it? That's no reason to risk the poor thing's life. I can't let you stick that spike in again.'

'How are you going to stop me?' I challenge him.

'Just by standing here,' he says. 'You'll have to wrestle me out of the way to get to the baby. If you do that, you'll almost certainly scratch me. That would mean my death. I don't think you'd kill me so recklessly.'

'I'm a zombie,' I say softly, moving closer, going up on my toes to give him the evil eye. 'You don't know how my mind works, what I'd do if pushed.'

'Perhaps,' he says. 'But I'm willing to take that chance. This baby needs our help and love. It's our duty to study it, protect it, nurse it back to health. It can talk, so perhaps it can answer our questions when it recovers, tell us where it came from, what it is.'

'The babies never wanted to discuss much in my dreams,' I sniff. 'They only wanted to slaughter me.'

'But this isn't a dream,' Timothy says. 'The baby simply reacted the way any cornered creature would. Look at it lying there now, helpless as a ... well, as a *baby*. It doesn't pose a threat to us.'

I shake my head stubbornly. 'It's a monster. Of course it poses a threat.'

'You're a monster too,' Timothy smiles. 'But I'm not afraid of you and I'm not afraid of the baby either. We can be its foster parents.'

I stare at him oddly. 'What, become a couple?'

'Of course not,' he smiles. 'But we could be partners and raise it together.'

'Why would I want to do that?'

'Salvation,' he says softly, stepping aside when he sees me hesitate. 'My paintings have kept me busy, and I plan to carry on doing them for as long as I can. But I lost a lot that defined me as a human when the world fell. Maybe this baby is a way for me to retrieve some of my humanity, and for you too.

'I haven't been truly happy since the zombies took control. Content, yes, with my artistic output, but happy? No. I don't think you're happy either. This is a chance for us to put the darkness behind us for a while.'

'What if you're wrong?' I croak. 'What if the baby's as monstrous as it looks and only drags us further into trouble?'

Timothy shrugs. 'Isn't it worth taking that risk?'

I have a clear line of attack now. If I darted at the baby, Timothy wouldn't be able to stop me. I could smash its skull with the spike, crush its throat, rip it to pieces.

But how could I live with myself if I did that to a baby? I've sunk lower than I ever dreamt I could, murdered, scraped heads bare of their brains, lived among the fetid and the damned. But to butcher a baby just because I'm afraid of it, because I had nightmares about things like it when I was younger ...

'That freak will be the ruin of us both,' I pout.

'Perhaps,' Timothy grins, understanding from my expression that I can't follow through on my threat. 'But we have to take that chance. Now let's see what we can do to help this poor lamb. Maybe it will stop screaming if we put it back in its cot, tend to its wound and show that we mean no harm. I'm sure that with a little TLC it will respond to our ministrations and –'

Timothy stops. He had started to bend to pick up the baby, but now he turns and stares at the doorway, into the gloom of the large room beyond. He cocks his head and frowns.

'Do you hear that?' he whispers.

'What?'

I step up beside him, trying to focus. The screams of the baby – '*mummy. mummy. mummy.*' – fill my head and I find it hard to tune them out.

Timothy moves through the doorway as if sleepwalking, eyes wide, a slight tic in his left cheek. I follow and close the door behind me, muffling the sounds of the baby.

I zone in on the new noises. They're coming from outside the building. Loud, scratching sounds, similar to a nail being dragged across a blackboard, only much sharper, and not one nail but dozens at the same time.

'What is it?' I ask softly, although part of me has already guessed. I'm not stupid. As I've stated proudly on more than one occasion in the past, I can put two and two together.

'Zombies,' Timothy says and his expression never alters. 'They've heard the baby. They're climbing the walls.' He points to the boarded-over windows with a surprisingly steady finger. Unlike the thick boards nailed over the windows on the ground floor, those up here were designed primarily to keep in the light, not keep out the ranks of the living dead. With all the oversized windows in this place, that would be impossible. This is a gallery, not a fortress. Anonymity was its only real defence.

'They know that we're here,' Timothy says. 'They're going to break in.'

And with those few calm words he pronounces his death sentence.

EIGHTEEN

'We have to get out of here!' I roar. 'Where are the exits?'

Timothy shakes his head wordlessly. He's staring at the boards covering the windows. He looks more thoughtful than scared.

'Timothy!' I scream, wanting to grab and shake him, but afraid of piercing his skin with my bones.

'The roof,' he murmurs.

'No good,' I grunt. 'They're climbing the walls. They can get to us in seconds on the roof. We have to go down to the ground floor, escape out the back, try to lose them on the streets.'

The first zombies start pounding on the glass and it shatters. They tear into the boards, ripping them loose. I catch glimpses of bones, fingers, faces, fangs.

Windows run the whole length of this room. The boards on pretty much all of them begin to crack and snap beneath the strain. There must be dozens of zombies out there, maybe more.

'Come on,' I shout, heading for the stairs.

'The baby,' Timothy says.

'You've got to be bloody joking!'

'The baby,' he says, stubbornly this time. 'I won't leave it to them.'

'You can't save it,' I growl. 'Its cries are what's drawing them. If we take it with us, they'll follow the noise.'

'But it's a baby . . .' he says miserably.

'No baby of our world,' I snort, then run with a wild idea. 'Maybe one of the zombies is its mother. That might explain why it looks so strange. She might have been pregnant when she was turned. Maybe it was born after she died.'

'That sounds feasible,' Timothy nods.

'If that's the case, they might accept it as their own. It might find a home with them.'

'Or they might rip it to shreds,' Timothy notes glumly. 'Maybe zombies stuck the spike through its head in the first place.'

I roll my eyes. 'Either way, the baby's going to be theirs in a minute. We can't stop them. We can put up a pointless fight and get torn apart or focus on our own necks and maybe make it out of here. Your choice, Timothy. I already died once. If they kill me again, it's not that big a deal.'

I wait for him to make up his mind. I'll stick by him no

matter what he decides. He's my friend and I want to do whatever I can to protect him, even though I know I can't.

Timothy licks his lips, torn between wanting to be a hero and knowing his limits. There's a loud snapping noise and the first of the zombies tumbles through the broken boards.

'God forgive us!' Timothy cries and races for the stairs, leaving the screeching baby to whatever fate has in store for it.

We pound down the stairs, taking them two or three at a time. I'm in agony, my broken ribs digging into my flesh and organs with every lurching movement. I ignore the pain as best I can, trying to focus on Timothy and getting him out of here before the zombies catch up.

We race through the room of blank canvases and supplies, the sound of the snapping boards above following us like the beat of tom-toms.

'Almost there,' Timothy pants, overtaking me as I stumble. 'There's a door at the rear of the building which I earmarked for an eventuality such as this. It opens quickly and quietly. If we can get outside, there's a good chance we can –'

He stops.

'Keep going,' I snap. 'This is no time to –'

I stop too.

We've come to a short set of steps. They lead to the main downstairs room, a huge, open space. The windows

128

at this level were boarded over professionally to keep out zombies. This should be the safest room in the entire building.

It's not.

The boards have held. So has the front door. But there are other doors. I'm sure that Timothy and the people who occupied this building before he came here did all that they could to secure those entrances. But there must have been a weak link somewhere, a chain that snapped, a lock that broke, hinges that crumbled.

Because the room is thick with zombies.

They stand silently, an army of them, motionless, faces raised to the ceiling, as if trying to determine exactly where the shriek of the baby is coming from.

Timothy trembles, losing his cool at last.

'Easy,' I whisper. 'They're not moving. They look like they're in some kind of a trance. We might be able to slip through them.'

I take a step down.

No response.

Another step.

Not a single zombie moves.

A couple more, then I stretch out my right foot to take the final step.

As soon as my toes touch the ground, the neck of every zombie snaps down as they lower their heads in perfect timing. They bare their teeth and snarl, then surge towards us without breaking ranks.

'Bugger!' I scream, turning to start back up the stairs. 'Come on!' I roar at Timothy. 'We've got to try for the roof.'

'We'll never make it,' he sobs but tears along after me.

We hurry through the room of supplies. Timothy is praying aloud, his words coming fast and furious, sounding like gibberish. We reach the stairs to the main gallery. They're clear. No sign of any zombies. I silently thank God and ask Him for another minute, sixty seconds, that's all we need. If we can make it to the roof, Timothy can cling to my back and I can either leap to another roof or all the way to the ground. My legs should be able to take a drop like that. I might break a few bones but it won't scramble my brain. Even if I can't carry on, Timothy can escape by himself. The zombies won't harm me once he's gone. He can return for me later. A minute. That's all we need. That's not too much to ask for, is it?

Apparently it is.

We're not even halfway up the stairs when the zombies from the upper floor come spilling towards us. They've made it through the windows and boards. They stagger down the steps, arms outstretched, leering hungrily.

Timothy screams and turns to flee, but more zombies are coming up the steps, having tracked us from the room below.

We're screwed.

I reach out to grab Timothy and pull him in tight, meaning to bite his neck, figuring the best I can do for him now is to end it quickly and maybe give him a chance of revitalising. I was injected with Dr Oystein's vaccine when I was a child. That's why I recovered my wits when I was turned into a zombie. Maybe I can pass some of my revitalising genes on to Timothy. I doubt he stands much of a chance but it's better than none at all.

But I'm too late. A zombie tackles me before I can strike and I fall to the steps, driven down by the weight of my assailant. Others throw themselves on top of me, burying me at the bottom of a pile of bodies.

'Timothy!' I shriek.

'Goodbye, B,' he says sadly as the first of the zombies pins him to the wall and scrapes at his stomach. Others swarm around him, digging into the flesh of his arms and legs with their bony fingers. Timothy screams, a cry of pure agony and loss. He screams again as zombies rip chunks of flesh from his body with their teeth. They're not concerned about converting him — they want to finish him off.

Madness fills Timothy's eyes, but with a supreme effort he shrugs it off for one last instant and locks gazes with me as I stare at him helplessly from my position on the floor.

'Take care of my paintings,' he wheezes pleadingly.

Then a zombie digs its fingers through Timothy's eyes.

He has time to scream once more before the zombie breaks through to his brain and starts scraping it out and cramming pieces into its foul, eager mouth.

There's no more screaming after that. Timothy Jackson is dead and gone. And all I can do is wait for the zombies to rip me apart and maybe send my soul to join Timothy's in the peaceful, welcome realms beyond.

NINETEEN

The zombies piled on top of me poke and maul me, unable to strike cleanly because so many are pressed in around me. Then, as the others retreat from Timothy's bloody, shredded remains, those holding me down fall still. I hear them sniffing and I sense them cocking their heads, listening for a heartbeat. When they realise I'm dead, they go slack and start pushing themselves off me, no longer viewing me as either a threat or a tasty treat.

I rise with a groan, prop myself against the wall and stare miscrably at all that is left of my artistic, eccentric friend. He was a crazy but sweet guy. He deserved better than this. But then so did billions of others. In this world of savagery and death, there's only what you get. *Deserve* doesn't come into it any more.

The zombies don't budge. Those with nothing to eat aren't moving at all, just standing on the steps, faces raised again, looking towards the top of the stairs. They're all silent, motionless, eyes fixed on the same spot. It's eerie.

I think about trying to slip away, but they reacted aggressively the last time I did that. I figure it's safer to give it some time, see what happens.

I don't have to wait long. After about a minute, the zombies part, moving to both sides of the stairs, forming a bizarre guard of honour. They don't lower their heads as they shuffle over, gazes fixed on that same spot at the top of the stairs.

This is really freaking me out. I ready myself to run, sod the consequences. I'd rather be torn apart than remain among this lot. There's something sinister going down and I don't want to be here when it hits.

But I'm too late. Even as I'm stretching out my foot to take my first tentative step, a pack of zombies appears at the top of the stairs. They march three abreast. They're holding their arms above their heads, linked together. Those at the front are children, then women, then men, arranged according to height, the way they would be if marching in a parade.

The children pass me, two rows of them. Then the women, three rows. Then the men start to come past. The first half-dozen have their arms linked over their heads, the same as the women and children. So have the men in the last two rows. But those between are holding something up high, as if it was a holy relic. Except this is no religious arte-fact.

It's the cot from the baby's room.

As they draw level with me, the procession comes to a stop. I'm staring at the side of the cot. As I watch, the baby crawls to the bars, then pulls itself up until it's standing. It looks calmer than it did before, a slight smile in place. It's stopped screaming. Its unblinking eyes are white again, the red sheen having receded.

The baby is looking at me.

'What the hell are you?' I moan.

'*mummy,*' the baby says softly.

'No,' I wheeze, shaking my head, denying the claim. 'I'm not your mother. I'm nothing to you.'

The baby's expression doesn't alter, but its hands move and it pulls the bars further apart, as if they were made of rubber. When the space is wide enough, the baby gently pokes its head through the gap. Its smile spreads.

'*join us mummy,*' it says in its tinny, unnatural voice.

'No,' I say again. My throat has tightened. If I could cry, I'd be weeping now.

The baby frowns. '*don't be frightened mummy. you're one of us. come with us mummy.*'

'I'm not one of you!' I scream. 'I don't even know what the hell you are.'

The baby giggles. '*yummy mummy. come.*'

'I'm not coming anywhere,' I snarl. 'You're a bloody freak. I wouldn't spit on you if you were on fire.'

The baby seems to consider that. After a long pause, it draws its head inside the cot and bends the bars back into place. It looks disappointed.

The zombies start to move again, down the stairs. The baby turns its face away and I think it's over. Then they stop. The baby's neck swivels and its nightmarish features swim back into view. Remembering the dreams I used to have, I expect it to tell me that I have to die now. I brace myself, waiting for the baby to climb the bars and hurl itself at me from the top of the cot.

But this baby doesn't appear to have murder on its mind. Its eyes don't redden and its mouth doesn't split into a vicious sneer. In fact it looks sad, maybe even lonely. And when it addresses me again, it's not to threaten or scare me. Instead it whispers something that makes me gawp at it with bewilderment.

'*we love you mummy.*'

With that, the macabre infant faces forward. It looks like a tiny prince or princess on a very grand throne, borne along by a team of devoted courtiers. It giggles, then the zombies resume their march. At the bottom of the stairs they process through the room of supplies, then down the small set of stairs to the ground-floor room and the exit.

The zombies around me hold their position until the

retinue passes from sight. Then they fall in behind and follow the cot and its carriers out of the building. A minute later, every single one of them has gone, and all that's left behind are the paintings, Timothy's scattered remains and the most incredulous, slack-jawed girl the world has ever seen.

TWENTY

For a long time I don't move. I don't even slump to the floor to take the weight from my weary legs. I'm frozen in place, replaying the scene in an endless loop inside my head, remembering everything about the baby, its face, what it said, how the zombies around it reacted.

It was controlling them. It called for them when I removed the spike. They came in their hundreds, rescued it, took it wherever it told them to take it. Like the mutants who work for Mr Dowling, the baby somehow has the power to make zombies do what it wants.

But it didn't have the power to bend *me* to its will. I was able to resist its call to follow it back to its lair.

Or was I? Maybe it simply let me go. It called me its mummy. It said it loved me. Maybe it thinks I really am its mother. It might have the potential to control me, but chose not to exercise it because of the bond it believes we share.

This is insane.

This is impossible.

This is terrifying.

Eventually I force myself to move. I struggle back up the stairs, taking them one slow step at a time. I shuffle into the nursery and gaze at the toys, the mobiles, the space where the cot stood. I spot the spike on the floor and seriously think about picking it up and driving it through my own skull. Escape from this world of horrors tempts me more than ever before. How can I witness something like this and carry on as if all is well or can ever be made well again?

Ultimately I reject suicide, fearful that it might not achieve anything. The baby and its clones originally tormented me in my dreams. Now they've chased me into this world. Who's to say they couldn't follow me into the afterlife too?

I limp back down the stairs to the room of supplies and search for a bag. I find a suitable one without too much difficulty, empty it of its contents, then retrace my steps and gather up the remains of poor Timothy. I hate having to do this – it would be much simpler to just leave – but I feel like I owe him. I brought the zombies down upon him. If I hadn't come here, he might never have tried to pull the spike from the baby's head. He could have gone on living and painting for months, maybe years, until his luck ran out. He's dead because of me. The least I can do is tend to his remains and give him some sort of a halfway decent burial.

I pick up every last scrap of Timothy, clothes as well as bones, skin and organs. I bag them all. After a while, I realise I'm making a low moaning noise, the closest I can get to crying. I don't make myself stop.

Job complete, I start to drag the bag down the stairs. I pause when I spot the trail of blood that I'm leaving behind. The bag isn't blood-proof. The bits inside are leaking.

I find another couple of bags, more resistant to liquids than the first, and triple-bag the corpse. That does the trick. There are no stains now.

I lug the grisly package to the front door, then climb the stairs once more, get a bucket of water and a mop and go to work on washing away the blood. Timothy's last request was that I looked after his paintings. The blood would attract flies and insects, maybe larger creatures like rats, which might attack the canvases. If I survive long enough, I plan to come back here every month or so, dust and clean, take care of the paintings, do all that I can to maintain the legacy of Timothy Jackson. That probably won't prove much of a comfort to him where he's gone, but it's all I can do to honour his memory.

When I'm finished cleaning, I return to the bag by the door and sit beside it. I don't want to go out until night has passed and day has dawned. Too many zombies at large in the darkness. Too many shadows in which the living dead and killer babies can hide.

I spend the night silently thinking, re-examining the world, my life, the very nature of the universe.

I thought I had it sussed. I told Burke, Rage and Timothy that this wasn't a world of miracles. If God existed, He didn't get involved in what was happening to us. I couldn't see His hand at work anywhere. We were on our own, I was sure of it.

The baby suggests to me that I was wrong. For years I dreamt of babies just like this one. They looked the same, wore the same clothes, had the same eyes and fangs, even said the same things.

'join us mummy.'

'don't be frightened mummy.'

'you're one of us.'

How could I have dreamt about them, never having seen such a demonic baby until tonight? How could my nightmares have been so accurate, correct down to the tiniest detail? Did God send me visions of the future, to prepare me for what was to come, so that I would realise He was real and put my faith in others that He had chosen? Does He want me for His team?

I don't know. I want to believe – it would be so wonderful to think that I understood everything, and had been hand-picked by such a powerful being – but I can't, not a hundred per cent. What I can do, however, after my run-in with the baby, is doubt. Not Dr Oystein but myself. There are enough questions in my mind now to make me far less sure that the doctor is deluded. I'm not saying I'm taking him at his word about God speaking to him. But I'm willing to listen to him now, to give him a chance, to put my faith in him.

Hell, from where I'm standing after my experiences tonight, it makes as much sense as anything else in this wickedly warped world.

TWENTY-ONE

The sun rises and I haul Timothy's remains outside. I shut the door behind me and hide the keys in the yard of the old brewery. I only remember the other door – the one the zombies used to get into the building – on my way down Brick Lane. I wince and think about retrieving the keys, going back inside and searching for the other entrance, to seal it.

'Sod it,' I mutter. 'Life's too short.'

I'll do my best for Timothy's paintings, but I'm not going to go overboard. Right now I'm exhausted. I'm not in my worst ever physical state – that was after Trafalgar Square – but mentally I'm beat. I reckon I need to spend at least a month in a Groove Tube to recover. I can't face even the minor challenge of searching for an open door. I'll do it the next time I come. If zombies or other intruders beat me to the punch, sneak in before I return and wreak havoc, tough.

I know where I want to take Timothy. I can't be sure but

I think he'd like it. Too bad if he doesn't because he can't complain now.

I lug the bag through the streets, shivering and straining, itching beneath the sun — I have my hoodie pulled up but I forgot the hat and jacket. It should be a short walk – no more than five or ten minutes any normal time – but it takes me half an hour. I don't mind. I'm not in a rush.

Finally I reach my destination. Christ Church Spitalfields, one of London's most famous churches, always popping up in films and TV shows about Jack the Ripper. It's a creepy place, but beautiful in a stark way, and I think Timothy would have appreciated it. He loved the East End. I don't recall him mentioning Christ Church, but I'm confident he would have raved about it if the subject had come up.

There's a small, grassy area in front of the church, some headstones dotted about. I find a nice spot for Timothy, somewhere that looks like it gets a lot of sun, then go in search of a shovel. I find one in a shop in Spitalfields Market, a colourful designer spade for ladies who wanted to look chic in their garden. There are no zombies in any of the shops or restaurants. I suppose they abandoned their resting places in response to the baby's call.

It takes me longer than I thought to dig the hole, and not just because I'm so drained. Digging a grave is hard work. I wouldn't have liked to do this for a living in the old days. I go down a couple of metres, not wanting to take chances and come back this way to find the grave dug up and raided by wild animals or zombies. When I'm happy with the depth, I haul myself out and lie on the grass for a while, an arm thrown across my face to shield my eyes from the sunlight.

Rising, I consider removing Timothy's remains from the bags, but why bother? Let them serve as his coffin. Probably not the way he would have liked to be buried, but better than nothing.

I lower the bags into the grave, then stand over it hesitantly, trying to think of the proper prayers to say.

'Ashes to ashes, dust to dust,' I murmur, but I can't remember the rest, and that doesn't seem like enough. In the end I recite a few *Hail Marys* and an *Our Father*.

'I hope you can carry on painting in the next world,' I conclude weakly, then fill in the grave, silently bid Timothy one last farewell and glance at the spire of Christ Church. Shivering, I wonder if there really is a God or if I'm just grasping at straws, if the babies of my nightmares actually were a sign or just some freakily incredible coincidence. Am I right to trust Dr Oystein, or am I making the worst mistake of my life?

With no way to know for sure, I shiver again, then turn my back on the church and shuffle along. I've spent enough time on the dead. Time to return to the business of the living and those caught in-between.

TWENTY-TWO

I make my way west, along the north bank of the river, no delays, no detours, no sightseeing. It's early afternoon when I cross Westminster Bridge and catch sight of County Hall. Nowhere has ever looked so inviting or felt so much like home, not even my old flat where I lived with Mum and Dad.

I don't beat about the bush. Ignoring the high-pitched noises coming out of the speakers dotted around the place – they deter normal zombies, but not a girl on a mission like me – I hobble down Belvedere Road, let myself into the building and make straight for Dr Oystein's small lab, where the Groove Tubes are housed. I have a feeling I'll find him there, and I'm right. He's working on something when I enter without knocking, running tests, studying the contents of a test tube.

The doctor doesn't look up, unaware that his privacy has

been disturbed. I don't announce myself. Instead I strip and dump my clothes on the floor, then limp to the nearest Tube, smiling warmly at the thought of immersing myself and blissing out, of emerging whole and fresh in a few weeks.

There's a ladder close to the Groove Tube. I climb up and in. I hold on to the sides of the cylinder, half submerged. I think about saying nothing, grinning as I imagine the perturbed look on Dr Oystein's face when he turns from his work later and spots me. But I can't hold my tongue.

'Doc,' I call.

The doctor looks up and his eyes widen. '*B?*' he gasps.

I smirk at him, let go of the sides and slip beneath the surface of the liquid. As I'm falling, just before I go under, I shout out playfully — 'I'm in!'

To be continued ...

THE
ZOM-B
CHRONICLES III
ZOM-B GLADIATOR

THEN . . .

Zombies ripped Becky Smith's heart from her chest and turned her into an undead, brain-munching beast. But several months later she recovered her senses and became a revitalised, a rare member of the undead who could think and control her cannibalistic urges.

Death was far harder for B than life had ever been. First she was held prisoner in an underground complex with a pack of teenaged revitaliseds. With the exception of B and one other, Rage, they were all fried by soldiers with flamethrowers when a killer clown invaded the complex and started a riot.

B broke free of the underground lair and found a London she barely recognised. Zombies had taken over. The few humans she crossed paths with all seemed as vicious as their undead foes—a hunter called Barnes and his posse slaughtered zombies for fun, a rifle-packing group on

HMS *Belfast* opened fire on anything that came within range, while the deranged clown and his mutant army spread terror and carnage wherever they set foot.

She finally found refuge in County Hall, a massive building behind the London Eye. A century-old zombie, Dr Oystein, had set up base there and was offering sanctuary to any revitalised who asked it of him. He had also recruited a few humans, such as Billy Burke, B's former teacher, and Reilly, a soldier and one of her captors in the underground complex.

Dr Oystein believed he was on a mission from God. He said that the clown B had encountered, the chilling and crazy Mr Dowling, worked for the Devil. If Dr Oystein and his zombie Angels didn't defeat Mr Dowling and his mutants, the last remaining survivors in the world would fall and Satan would claim their souls.

B thought the doctor was insane. Although she feared being alone, and was worried about what would happen next, she turned her back on County Hall and left to find somewhere else in the city to call home.

She ended up in the studio of Timothy Jackson, an artist who spent his days painting what he saw on the streets of zombie-infected London. Timothy took her to meet a strange baby which he had found. It was sexless and monstrous. A spike was sticking out of its head and it hadn't eaten in weeks, yet it was still somehow alive.

When B removed the spike, the baby screamed for help and dozens of zombies responded to its call. They flocked to the studio, broke in, killed Timothy and made off with the baby, but not before it had asked B to accompany them. It called her its mummy and said she was one of them.

B refused to go with the inhuman baby and its undead coterie. But her world was changed, as was her opinion of Dr Oystein and his claim to be in contact with God. Because B had dreamt of babies like this one when she was alive. In her dreams they had looked exactly like this child, behaved the same way, said the same things. And, despite her scepticism, B had to conclude that a higher power must have sent her the dreams as a warning, to prepare her for this day and provide her with the evidence she'd need in order to accept Dr Oystein's far-fetched claims.

B returned to County Hall, pledged herself to Dr Oystein then hopped into one of his body-reviving Groove Tubes to restore her sharpness and strength, so that she would be fresh and ready for the war with Mr Dowling which was to come.

NOW ...

ONE

There's a tunnel beneath Waterloo Station that used to be a haven for graffiti artists. Anyone was allowed to paint whatever they wanted on the walls, floor or ceiling.

The zombies put a stop to the artists with their stencils and spray paint, but the art remains, bright, bold and colourful. It covers every inch of the tunnel. If humans ever eliminate the undead and take control of the world again, I bet a lot of people will come to this place to admire the paintings.

But I'm not here today for the graffiti.

I'm here for the zombies.

We usually keep this tunnel clear of the living dead. It's easily done. Zombies have sensitive ears. High-pitched noises cut through our skulls and make our teeth shake. When Dr Oystein moved into County Hall, he placed speakers in hidden places around the area and played a loop of sharp noises through them, guaranteed to send any zombie within range running for cover. It keeps the drooling, brain-hungry riff-raff from our door.

But we haven't been playing the loop in the tunnel for the last few nights. We wanted company and figured the dark, quiet space would draw a crowd once we cut the power to the speakers.

We figured right. There are twenty-five or thirty zombies in residence, a mix of men, women and kids, some in suits or nice dresses, others in more casual wear, a few naked or as good as. Blank expressions, long, sharp teeth, bones sticking out of their fingers and toes, wisps of green moss wherever they were bitten or cut when they were alive.

I study the zombies with a touch of nerves, but no disgust, revulsion or pity. They're my own kind. Except for the fact that my brain works, I'm no different to them.

I'm part of a group of six. The others are the same as me, revitalised Angels, soldiers in Dr Oystein's undead army. Carl Clay stands to my left, looking impeccable in his top-of-the-range, designer gear. Ashtat Kiarostami is to my right, dressed in a blue, loose-fitting suit, with a white headscarf. The bulky Rage is on the other side of Carl, wearing the leathers that he's favoured since his time as a zom head. Shane Fitz and Jakob Pegg are next to Ashtat, Shane looking as yobbish as ever in a tracksuit and with a gold chain dangling from his neck, Jakob pale and sickly in a pair of jeans and a shirt that sags on his bony frame.

We're all unarmed.

'Do you think there are enough of them?' Carl asks, frowning as he counts the zombies.

'Five to one,' Shane sniffs. 'Those are long enough odds for me. How many more do you want to face?'

'There aren't many men among them,' Carl notes.

'Are you suggesting that women are inferior?' Ashtat asks coldly.

Carl winces. 'No. But generally speaking they're not as strong as men. It's the way of the world. You can't argue with that.'

'In life, no,' Ashtat says. 'But death levels the playing field. I have noticed no real difference between the sexes in our battles so far. Muscles are not the factor they once were, not in reviveds. Or revitaliseds,' she adds pointedly.

Carl makes a sighing sound, which isn't easy when you don't have functioning lungs. 'All right. I don't want an argument. Are we all happy to press ahead? We don't want to wait another day in case more of them come to seek shelter here?' He looks around and everyone shrugs or nods. 'Fair enough. We'll crack on. How about you, Reilly? Are you ready?'

The soldier is standing behind us. He's not a happy bunny.

'I can't believe I let Zhang talk me into this,' he mutters. He's sweating. That's something no revitalised could ever mimic. The walking dead don't sweat.

'Don't be a baby,' Rage grins. 'We've all got to be prepared to make sacrifices for the cause.'

'Yeah?' Reilly snarls. 'What have *you* sacrificed lately?'

'My sense of compassion,' Rage snaps. 'Now quit moaning or we'll leave you here by yourself. Are you ready or not?'

'I suppose,' Reilly mutters miserably. He's really not enjoying this. I don't blame him. It can't be easy, placing your life in the hands of a surly shower of teenage zombies.

Ashtat and I nudge apart and Reilly steps through the gap. He's covered himself from the neck down in thick leathers and he's wearing a helmet with a tough glass visor. The gear won't protect him for long if a zombie gets hold of him and rips in, but it should guard him against casual swipes, spit and flying blood.

Reilly moves a couple of metres ahead of us, gulps, then calls out loudly, 'I don't suppose any of you creeps have seen Banksy?'

The zombies didn't pay much attention to us when we filed in. They could tell from our moss-covered wounds and the bones jutting out of our fingertips that we were in the same boat as them.

Reilly is a whole different kettle of fish. When he shouts,

they jerk to attention and lock their sights on him. They note his covered form, his shaky grin behind the visor. They clock his heartbeat. They smell his blood, fresh and pure, his sweat, the scent of the food he ate that morning on his lips and tongue, his juicy brain.

The zombies howl with glee and hunger, a penetrating, fearsome sound. Then they move as one and surge towards us, fingers flexing, teeth gnashing, primed, deadly assassins whose only purpose in this world is to attack and tear asunder.

It's killing time!

TWO

We dart ahead of Reilly and tackle the onrushing zombies. I run into a woman who is wearing a bra and knickers and nothing else. There are curlers in her hair. Looks like the living dead caught her at home when she was getting ready to go out.

I strike swiftly at the woman, a flurry of blows to her face and neck. She snarls and tries to hit back. I turn quickly, raising my leg high, and kick the back of her head as I spin. She's slammed sideways. I'm on her instantly. Making the fingers of my right hand straight and hard, I drive the bones sticking out of them down sharply into her skull, piercing the covering of bone, digging into the vulnerable brain beneath.

The woman shudders, makes a low moaning noise, then falls still. I withdraw my hand and leave her to lie in the dust of the tunnel, truly dead now.

A man is rushing past me, hands outstretched, reaching for Reilly. I elbow him in the ribs. I can't knock the wind out of his sails – there's no wind in them to begin with – but the force of the blow sends him off course. As he staggers, I follow after him, fingers ready to crack open another head and rid the city of one more zombie.

I don't like doing this. I refused to kill reviveds when I was a prisoner in the military complex. But Dr Oystein has convinced me that it's necessary. If we are to triumph in the war to come, we need to sharpen ourselves in combat. So, as much as I hate it, I kill as ordered, but I do it quickly and cleanly, not wanting to torment these poor lost souls.

The other Angels are busy around me. Each of us has a different ability and we've all been trained by Master Zhang to focus on our strengths. We've been told to test specific skills today, to only deviate from them if absolutely necessary. Mine is the speed with which I can strike—I have quick hands and feet, very nimble.

Ashtat is our pack's version of the Karate Kid. She whirls gracefully around the tunnel, chopping and kicking, leaping high into the air to casually swing a foot at a man's head—a second later it's been knocked clear of his neck. She lands smoothly, pounces after the head, comes down on it with a well-placed heel to squish the brain and put the zombie out of action.

Rage is a one-man wrecking machine. He's the strongest

of us all. He lets his opponents get close, then clubs them over the head or grabs them in a bear hug and squeezes until their brains seep out through their eye sockets and ear canals. He laughs and cracks jokes as he kills. He doesn't have any of the reservations that I do.

Posh Carl can jump like a grasshopper. He leaps around, landing among the reviveds, disrupting and scattering them, pushing them over or tripping them up, then springing across the tunnel to strike again. He could kill easily but he's been told not to. Today he's just here to confuse and disrupt.

Jakob isn't killing either. He's under orders to protect Reilly from any revived that gets past the rest of us. Jakob can run very fast. He's skinny and unhealthy-looking, even for a zombie, the result of the cancer he was dying from when he was turned. He's always in pain, but he can shrug it off when he has to. In the tunnel he stays focused, pulling Reilly away from stray zombies, ready to pick him up and run with him if something goes seriously wrong and the rest of us get into difficulties.

Ginger Shane's fingerbones and toe bones are tougher than anyone else's. We can all dig our bones into planks or crumbling bricks, but Shane can gouge a hole in a slab of concrete. He keeps climbing the walls and dropping on our opponents. He's laughing like Rage – the pair have become thick as thieves – until one of the zombies snags the gold chain around his neck and rips it loose.

'Not my chain!' Shane roars as it flies across the tunnel. He loses interest in the zombie and hurries after the keepsake.

'Shane!' Ashtat snaps. 'Don't abandon your position.'

'Get stuffed,' he grunts, shoving a zombie out of his way, scooping to reclaim his cherished possession.

A female zombie attacks him from the side as he's brushing dirt from the chain. He goes down with a cry of surprise. The woman tears at him, digs her fingers into his stomach, bites down hard on his left shoulder.

Shane roars and slaps the revived. He shouts for help. Ashtat curses and starts towards him, but Jakob is faster. Forgetting his orders, he abandons Reilly and races to the aid of his friend, tugging the zombie away, buying Shane time to get back on his feet.

'Where's my bloody guard gone?' Reilly bellows. Then, a second later, he moans, 'Oh crap.'

A couple of zombies have broken through and are bearing down on him. Reilly turns to run but the living dead are faster. One, a guy, grabs his waist. The other, a woman, tries to chew through his helmet.

For a second I freeze, imagining having to break Reilly's loss to Ciara, the always stylishly dressed dinner lady who fixes our meals at County Hall. The pair of living humans have recently started dating, after the shy Reilly finally worked up the courage to ask her out. He didn't tell her he was coming with us today. Didn't want her to worry.

Snapping back into action, I throw myself in Reilly's direction, praying I'm not too late. But Carl beats me to the punch. He leaps in out of nowhere, kicks the head of the woman chewing on Reilly's helmet, grabs the ears of her partner and tugs sharply. Zombies don't feel pain as much as the living, but we can be hurt. The man screeches and loses interest in Reilly. He bats Carl away, then dives after him.

The woman is back at Reilly's helmet again, but before she can bare her fangs and chow down, Ashtat is on her, kicking furiously, short, sharp jabs, forcing her to retreat.

I attack the undead man from behind. I thrust a hand into his back and out through his chest. His heart bursts and chunks drip from my fingers. That won't stop him – zombies can survive without any organ except their brain – but it sure as hell distracts him. He writhes like a speared fish, trying to tear free.

I hold firm, wrapping my other arm round him, jamming my face in close to his back to present less of a target for his flailing arms. As he struggles, Carl makes a blade of his fingers, takes aim, then sends his left hand shooting through the revived's right eye. He goes in up to his wrist, then sneers at the zombie as he stiffens and dies.

'That'll teach you to mess with the Clay.'

'Are you all right?' I shout at Reilly. He's patting himself, checking for rips in his leathers, features twisted frantically behind the visor. 'Reilly! Are you OK?'

'I think so,' he wheezes, starting to relax. 'I don't think I've been scratched. Where the hell is Jakob?'

'Helping Shane.'

Reilly growls. 'My boot's gonna be helping its way up his arse when I get him back to County Hall.'

'No swearing,' Rage crows as he grabs the head of a boy who can't be more than eight or nine years old. 'You'll set a bad example.'

'A lot of use you were,' I throw back at him.

Rage shrugs. 'Doesn't matter to me if Reilly gets turned. Just another monster for us to kill. The more the merrier as far as I'm concerned.'

I curse Rage, not for the first time, and stride towards him. 'Let the kid go,' I tell him, before he crushes the boy's skull.

'Why?' he laughs. 'Do you want to fight me?'

'No. But you know the rules—we need to check kids out before we destroy them.'

Rage scowls. 'I hate rules.'

'Tough. If you don't obey them, I'll tell Dr Oystein and we'll see how welcome you are at County Hall then.'

Rage mumbles something to himself, then lets the boy go. The kid immediately sets after Reilly, every bit as anxious to

169

sink his fangs into a living human's brain as the adults are. I tackle him and easily stop his charge. I pull out the cuffs which I've brought along especially for this and slip a pair on to his wrists. Letting go, I push him to the ground, then snap another pair shut around his ankles. As the boy struggles furiously to break free, mewling miserably, I assess the situation.

Shane is back in the thick of things. He looks ashamed and so he should. A sheepish Jakob has resumed his position and is protecting Reilly again. Ashtat and Rage are picking off the last few adult reviveds. Carl has cuffed a girl even younger than the boy and is moving in on the last remaining child, another boy, this one not far off my age.

It's plain sailing now.

A minute later every zombie has been dispatched except for the three kids. As the rest of the Angels brush themselves down and give each other high-fives, I examine the cuffed prisoners, searching their thighs and arms for c-shaped scars. Dr Oystein spent decades injecting children with a vaccine which would help them fight the zombie gene if infected. If we find any child with the mark, we take them back to County Hall in case they revitalise further down the line.

Sadly, none of these three bears the scar of hope. They're regular reviveds, damned from the moment they were turned. I steel myself, offer up a quick prayer, then finish them off one by one. I feel sick every time I do this. I know they're undead killers, no different to any of the adult zombies that I've put out of their misery, but it still feels wrong.

I could ask one of the others to do it – Rage has no qualms about ripping the brain from a young zombie's head – but this is a hard world and Master Zhang has warned us that each one of us needs to toughen up if we're going to thrive and be of use to Dr Oystein. So I grit my teeth and force myself to push through with the dirty deed. I just hope, if God is watching, that He understands and forgives me, though I'm not sure I'll ever be able to forgive myself.

'Nice work,' Rage says when I'm done. He offers me his hand to high-five but I ignore him.

'I'm going to take that chain and help Reilly shove it up your arse,' I bark at Shane.

'I screwed up,' he winces. 'I'm sorry. It won't happen again. But my dad gave me that chain. It's all I have left of either of my parents.'

'Bullshit,' Rage snorts. 'I saw you take it from a shop last week.'

The pair burst out laughing. 'You shouldn't have told her,' Shane giggles as I glower at him. 'I had her going. She'd have melted and pardoned me.'

'*I* wouldn't have,' Reilly snarls, removing his helmet. 'My bloody *life* was on the line. I haven't been vaccinated.

There's no coming back for me if I get turned. You risked my safety over a bloody chain that you can replace any time?'

Shane's smile fades. 'I really did screw up. I lost my head for a minute. I'm sorry, Reilly, honestly I am.'

'You'd better be,' Reilly says stiffly. 'And note this, you little thug—if anything like that happens again, I'll kill you. Even if I get bitten or scratched, I'll make it my job to stab you through the brain before I turn. Understand?'

Shane nods and averts his gaze.

'Apart from that, we did brilliantly,' Rage cheers, clapping loudly. 'Now let's go tell Master Zhang how we fared and ask Ciara to rustle us up some delicious brain stew. I don't know about you guys, but killing always makes me hungry.'

Rage licks his lips, the others laugh and cheer, then we trudge back to County Hall, experiment concluded, skills honed, one step closer to our hellish graduation.

THREE

We report back to Master Zhang, who's waiting for us in one of the rooms where he trains his recruits. He's angry when he hears what Shane and Jakob did. He's always stressing the need to focus and obey a direct order.

'No rest tonight,' he snaps at them. 'I want to see both of you here at lights out. I will work you through the night and it will not be a workout that you forget in a hurry.'

Shane pulls a face but Jakob only nods glumly.

'What about the others?' Zhang asks Reilly. 'Did they perform to your satisfaction?'

'Yeah. I don't have any complaints. They looked sharp.'

Our mentor sniffs, then waves us away. Shane hesitates. 'Master, I don't want to make a big deal of it, but I was injured. I think I might need a spell in a Groove Tube.'

'Let me see.' Zhang examines Shane's stomach and shoulder. The shoulder's no biggie, but the zombie dug quite deeply into the lining of his stomach. No guts are oozing out but it's bloody down there. 'Does it hurt?' Zhang asks.

'Yes,' Shane says.

'Good.' Zhang pokes one of the wounds and Shane cries out and doubles over. 'You will avoid the Groove Tubes. You will suffer your injuries and learn from the pain. Understand?'

'Yes ... Master,' Shane wheezes.

'Now get out of here, all of you,' Zhang says. 'I am expecting another group for training soon, and hopefully they will pay more attention to my instructions than you.'

We bow and take our leave. Shane limps along, gingerly massaging the flesh around his stomach. 'I bet the cuts get infected,' he mutters.

'It will serve you right if they do,' Ashtat says. 'You let us down and put Reilly's life in danger.'

'What about cancer boy?' Shane snaps. 'Jakob screwed up too.'

'Yes,' Ashtat says. 'But he screwed up trying to save a friend's life, not because he was worried about what would happen to an item of cheap jewellery.'

Shane glares at Ashtat and starts to retort.

'Leave it, big boy,' Rage chuckles, slapping Shane's back. 'They're right, you're wrong. Live with it, get over it, move on. Now, who's coming with me to get some stew?'

Everyone says they'll tag along with Rage, except me.

'I'm heading back to our room,' I tell them.

'Don't be a killjoy,' Carl frowns. 'Come with us. We did well in there apart from a couple of hiccups. Join the cele-brations.'

'No, you're all right, I'm fine.'

'Suit yourself,' Carl says, irritated. They head off in search of Ciara, a close, united pack of friends. I stare after them longingly, wishing I could belong, but at the same time knowing why I keep myself separate.

It's been a month since Dr Oystein fished me out of the Groove Tube after my fall from the London Eye and my run-in with the inhuman baby. When I'd dried off and he'd filed down my fangs and pumped my insides clean, I told him about my adventures, the monstrous baby and the dreams I'd had when I was alive of creatures just like it.

Dr Oystein is always hard to read, but my description of the baby didn't seem to come as a great shock. I think he already knew about the existence of such beings. My dreams, on the other hand, disturbed and intrigued him in equal measure. He made me recount them as clearly as I could.

'You are sure the babies in your nightmares were exactly the same as this one?' he asked. 'You are not imagining the similarity?'

'No,' I told him. 'I had the dreams all of my life, as far back as I can recall, until I was killed and stopped sleeping.

I'm sure this baby was the same, not just because of the way it looked, but how it spoke and what it said.'

I told the doc how Owl Man had asked about my dreams when he came to visit me before the zombie uprising. That troubled him even more.

'I did not know that you had seen our owl-eyed associate before your encounter in Trafalgar Square,' he murmured.

I shrugged. 'I never thought to mention that. It didn't seem important. Do you know who he is?'

The doc nodded.

'What's his name?'

'That is irrelevant.' He smiled. 'I actually prefer Owl Man—it suits him better. That is how I will refer to him from now on.'

I wanted to learn more about Owl Man and the babies, but Dr Oystein said it was not yet time.

'Please be patient. I will share all the information that I possess with you, as I vowed when you first came here, but you must trust me to fill in the blanks as I see fit. I want to think about this first, what the nightmares might signify, how they link in with everything else.'

I told him I thought that the dreams had been sent to me by some higher force, so I'd see there were hidden, inexplicable depths to the world, and be more inclined to believe that the doc was telling me the truth when I came here.

'If that is the case,' Dr Oystein said softly, 'there is more to you than I first suspected. None of the other Angels had such dreams when they were alive. If God shared a premonition with you, there must be a reason for it. Perhaps you have a crucial role to play in the war with Mr Dowling.'

'Is that a good thing?' I asked.

He made a low, rumbling noise. 'I cannot say for sure. I know only that such responsibility is a frightening prospect. I have had to deal with it for decades. I do not wish to scare you, but I have to say that I would not wish such a burden on anyone.'

Then he kissed my forehead tenderly and sent me back to my room, telling me that he would consider what I'd told him and do all that he could to help me comprehend my path and steer me along it as best he could.

FOUR

I return to my room, change clothes, then scan the books on my shelves. I don't have a lot of stuff. Spare clothes, an iPod, some video games, a few nice watches and the books. I don't feel the need to cram my share of the room with personal items. London is an open city these days. Any time I want anything, I can simply go out and find it.

The others are the same. Nobody has bothered to clutter up their shelves or store goods in the many niches of County Hall. Carl has lots of fancy gear because he's into fashion, Shane has stacks of gold chains because he thinks they're cool, and Ashtat has hundreds of boxes of matches which she uses to make her brilliantly detailed models—she's currently working on one of Canary Wharf, her most ambitious project yet. Jakob has virtually nothing apart from some small photos of his family which he found in his mother's purse after she'd been killed along with his dad and sister.

My books are all about art and sculpture. If you'd told me when I was alive that I'd one day be an avid reader of such volumes, I'd have sneered. But time drags here. It's fine when we're training or on a mission, but otherwise we're stuck inside, staring at the walls.

The others play games and watch movies, but I've been keeping myself distant from my fellow Angels. Films don't hold the same appeal for me as they used to. Video games are the same. I haven't ditched them completely, but I can't spend a lot of time on them. I still listen to music, but my ears are so sensitive that I have to play the songs low, and where's the fun in that?

Art, on the other hand, has started to appeal to me. Mum was big into art and often tried to pass on her love of it to me. I resisted, in large part because I knew that Dad was scornful of it. He thought artists were pretentious wasters and I didn't want him looking down his nose at me.

My encounters with Timothy Jackson changed my view. His drawings of zombies fascinated me and I found myself thinking about them, the styles he had adopted, how they worked in different ways. I studied his paintings for a long time, then visited a few galleries to compare them with the work of other artists.

I started looking through the books in gallery shops. I wouldn't have dared go into such places in the old days. I'd have been afraid that the staff would laugh at me, or think

I was just there to steal. But now there are only zombies to bear witness, and they couldn't care less about idle browsers.

I hadn't planned to read any of the books in detail, but the more I learnt, the more I could appreciate the pictures in them, as well as those hanging on the walls of the galleries. I lugged a couple of art books back to flick through, and soon my shelves started to fill up. There's no problem finding new volumes—here are loads of shops in London and they're open for business twenty-four hours a day, no credit card or cash required, and only the odd zombie bookseller or two to contend with.

Dr Oystein likes us to rest at night, to lie in our beds and act as if we're asleep. I read during that time, rather than just lie in the dark and count the seconds as they slowly tick by. No complaints from the others about my reading light—a few of them read as well, or play hand-held video games.

I used to be a slow reader but I've been speeding up recently. In the beginning I tended to choose books with lots of pictures in them, but now I've moved on to thick textbooks. I don't finish everything that I start, but when a book grabs my interest, I can plough through it pretty niftily.

So what am I in the mood for today? I study the titles, pick up a few, read the blurb on the back covers, then replace them. Until I come to *The Complete Letters of Vincent Van Gogh*. I don't recall bringing this back, and it's a monster, so I'm sure I would have remembered. Frowning, I slide it free of the books around it and a note falls out. It's from Carl.

I saw you reading a book about Van Gogh. My dad had a copy of this in his library and often raved about it. I thought you might like to give it a go. Let me know if it's any good and I might try it myself.

I scowl at the note. I don't like it when people do nice things for me. I never know how to react. I suppose I'll have to thank Carl now—if I don't, I'll look like a mean-spirited cow. Why couldn't he have just told me about the book and let me find it for myself? Bloody do-gooder.

I think about dumping the book in the bin, but that would make me look childish and ungrateful. Besides, Van Gogh *is* one of my favourite artists and it sounds like a good read. Grumbling softly, I head to bed and settle down for a few hours of solitary reading.

I quickly get into the letters and time flies by. Carl has picked a winner. On the one hand that annoys me, because it means I won't be able to jeer at him for giving me a piece of crap to read. But on the other hand I'm delighted to have discovered a brilliant new book, and I soon forget about Carl and having to say thank you and everything else.

A soft voice brings me back to the real world. 'I never thought I'd see B Smith lost in a book.'

I jump slightly – I had no idea that anyone had entered

the room – and glance up. It's my old teacher, Mr Burke, standing in the doorway, beaming at me. 'I've always had a soft spot for nutters who cut their ears off,' I growl, carefully closing the book and setting it aside. 'Besides, this is a great read. I might have studied harder if I'd been pushed towards these sorts of books in school.'

'No,' Burke laughs. 'You wouldn't have given it a chance. You were a busy girl, so many slacker friends, so many things not to do with them. They wouldn't have been impressed if you'd started reading books instead of hanging out with them on street corners.'

Burke crosses the room, picks up the book and flicks through it. He looks much older than he did in school, bags under his eyes, hair almost completely grey now. I never had a crush on Burke, but as teachers went, he was a bit of all right. Now he looks like a broken old man.

'I always meant to give this a try,' Burke says.

'You'd heard about it?'

'Yes. I was never much of an art buff. Biographies were my poison. *Seven Pillars of Wisdom*—now *that* was a book. But Van Gogh's letters were famous. I don't suppose I'll get time to read them now. I can't stay up all night like some undead people I can name.'

'I could always bite you,' I joke. 'Get Dr Oystein to vaccinate you first. You might turn into one of us. Then you can stay up as late as you like.'

'I've already been vaccinated,' Burke says, sitting on the bed next to mine, the one Jakob sleeps in.

'You have?' I sit upright and stare at him.

'I asked Dr Oystein to give me the shot not long after I started working for him.'

'Why?' I cry. 'You know what it means, don't you? Unless you get infected, the vaccine will attack your system and melt you down. You'll be dead within the next ten or fifteen years.'

Burke shrugs. 'It's unlikely I'll last that long. There's a far greater probability that I'll be snagged by a zombie. If they don't eat my brain and I turn, I'd like the chance to revitalise. I know most adults don't, but still, better some hope than none at all.'

I shake my head. 'And what if you don't get bitten or scratched?'

Burke smiles. 'Then I'll miss out on old age. I wasn't looking forward to it anyway. I'd rather go in my prime, young, virile and full of life.'

'Too late,' I mutter. 'You missed that boat years ago.'

Burke laughs out loud then leans forward. 'How have you been, B? I haven't seen much of you since you returned.'

It's my turn to shrug. 'Fine. I've settled in. Learning lots. Training hard. Doing my bit for the cause.'

'Have you been on a mission yet?'

'Only scouting or training missions close to County Hall.'

The Angels do a lot of routine scouting, searching the streets and buildings of London for survivors—if we find any, we offer them a safe home at County Hall. We're also on the lookout for Mr Dowling and his mutants, as well as any human soldiers who might be on patrol. And, of course, we hunt for brains. We need regular supplies if we're to stay in control of our senses. Certain Angels do nothing except scour hospitals, schools and public buildings in search of corpses whose skulls they can scrape clean of brains to bring back for the pot, but all of us are expected to pitch in to some extent. One of the less exciting chores which everyone has to share.

I like getting out of County Hall when we go scouting, but it's an unpleasant sensation at the same time because we never know what we're going to run into, if Mr Dowling or his mutants will pop up, or if human hunters will set their sights on us. I crossed swords with some of them before I found my way here, the American Barnes and his buddies. There are others, bored survivors who pass the time by notching up kills. Not that they consider it killing. I mean, zombies are already dead, so it's no big deal to them.

The others in my group have been on more serious missions, where they've escorted humans out of London, or gone into dangerous areas with orders to carry out specific tasks. But Rage and I haven't been allowed on any of those yet.

'What about in your down time?' Burke asks.

I nod at the book. 'I've been making up for all those years when I never read anything other than porn stories online.'

Burke blinks. 'You're joking, aren't you?'

'Nothing wrong with a bit of sauce,' I smirk.

'Only if you're an appropriate age,' Burke huffs.

'Don't get all grown-up on me,' I snap. 'I had unlimited access to the internet from the age of ten or eleven. You think I wasn't curious? You think anyone my age didn't have a look to see what all the fuss was about? It wasn't like when you were a kid. The world was our oyster. We could find out about anything.'

'I suppose,' he sighs, then smiles again. '*The world was our oyster.* You never used a phrase like that in the old days. All that reading must be rubbing off on you.'

'Of course it is. I'm not thick.'

'No,' Burke agrees. 'And never were. Even when you acted it.'

Burke picks up the book and looks at it closely again. He's obviously come to discuss something with me. I've an idea what it is but I don't say anything. I'm not going to make things easy for him. That's not my style.

'I don't want this to come out the wrong way,' Burke says hesitantly. 'And I'd hate to be classed as a teacher who ever discouraged reading. But are you maybe spending a bit too much time here on your own with your head stuck in a book?'

'No,' I answer shortly.

Burke chuckles, then sets the book aside and gets serious. 'What's wrong, B?'

'Nothing. I'm peachy.'

'No. You're not. Dr Oystein noticed and brought it to my attention.'

'Noticed what?'

'You returned to the fold after that incident with the baby,' Burke says, 'but you haven't made any effort to fit in with the other Angels. You don't socialise or hang out with your room-mates.'

'Maybe I don't like them,' I sniff.

'I doubt that's the case,' he says. 'If it was, you could simply ask to move in with a different group.'

'I thought that wasn't allowed. Dr Oystein tells us where to bed down.'

'When you first come here, yes. But if Ashtat and the others are still getting on your nerves after this much time, he'll be happy to let you switch. But they're not the problem, are they?'

'Rage is a pain,' I mutter.

'You don't get on with him?'

'I don't trust him. Never have, never will.'

'But the others?' Burke presses.

I shrug stiffly.

'If you tell me what's troubling you, I might be able to

help,' he says kindly. 'A problem is never as bad as it seems if you share it with a friend.'

'But I don't need a friend,' I mumble. 'I don't *want* one. I don't mind working with the Angels, but I don't want to make friends with them.'

'Why not?' Burke asks, surprised.

'I'd rather be alone,' I say quietly.

Burke frowns, trying to make sense of me.

'It's not that complicated,' I snicker.

'It is to me,' Burke says. 'I'd have thought that someone in your position would give anything to find a friend.'

'What's so bad about my position?' I bark.

'Well, you're undead,' he says. 'Living people want nothing to do with you. Regular zombies have no interest in you either. There aren't many people left who could ever be tempted to give a damn about you. If you spurn the advances of the Angels, you're unlikely to find a friend anywhere else.'

'But I just told you I don't want any friends,' I remind him.

'You must,' Burke insists. 'You can't want to be all alone in the world.'

'I bloody well do,' I snort.

'Why?'

'Because it's simpler that way.' I reconsider my words and try again. 'Because it's safer.' I look down at my hands, at the bones sticking out of my fingers, remembering the blood that has stained them. 'You weren't there in the school when the zombies attacked. You were off sick that day. You didn't see us as we raced for freedom. You didn't see so many of my friends die, Suze and Copper and Linzer and . . .

'You weren't there when Mr Dowling invaded the underground complex either. You didn't see the zom heads tear into Mark or hear their death screams when Josh caught up with them. You didn't smell their burning flesh in the air.

'You weren't with me when all those people were killed in Trafalgar Square. Or when Sister Clare and her supporters marched into the belly of Liverpool Street Station. Or when Timothy was butchered.'

'I've seen terrible things too,' Burke says sadly.

'I'm sure you have. But I've *only* seen terrible things since I regained my mind. I've found death everywhere I've turned, or death has found me. I'm not saying I'm a jinx— I don't think I'm that important. But this is death's world now and I've run into the Grim Reaper every time I've turned a corner or paused for breath. Well, not actual breath, obviously, but you get the picture.'

I meet Burke's gaze at last. 'Pretty much everyone I've known and cared about has died or been taken from me. I'm sick of it. I don't want to endure the pain again. The Angels will be killed, I'm sure of it. Dr Oystein will get ambushed by Mr Dowling and his mutants. You'll be turned or slaughtered. It will all go tits up somewhere along the line.

'I don't want to feel anything when that happens. I don't want to lose friends or loved ones. I want to be able to get on with things and find somewhere else to hole up until death swings by again. I'd rather be a loner than feel lonely.'

Burke's eyes fill with pity. 'B . . .' he croaks.

'Don't,' I stop him. 'You came for answers and I've given them to you. Now leave me alone. It's all I ask of you. It's all I ask of anyone.'

Then I pick up the book, open it and stare at the words until Burke gets up and silently slips away, leaving me by myself. Not the way I like it really. Just the way it has to be if I'm not going to go crazy and lose myself to grief and madness in this harsh, unforgiving abattoir of a world.

FIVE

Getting ready to head out on another scouting mission. I was hoping Master Zhang would give us something meatier to deal with, but no, it's just another sweep of the area, this time around Covent Garden. There are lots of streets set back from the market, crammed with flats. We've been through there before, but repetition is nothing new.

We don't take any weapons when we head out, but we dress in heavy clothes and gloves to protect our skin from the sun. We also slap on loads of suntan lotion. Our clothes have been individually prepared for us, holes cut away to reveal our wounds and the wisps of green moss which signify to other zombies that we're undead like them.

I study the hole in my chest as I twist my jacket round. I've got so used to it that I can't really remember what it was like before. I hated being one tit short of a full set to begin with. Now I couldn't give a toss.

'I have said it before but I will say it again,' someone murmurs behind me. 'You are a most remarkable example of a zombie, Becky Smith.'

I turn, smiling, to face Dr Oystein. The doc never changes much. He favours a light grey suit, neatly ironed white shirt and a snazzy tie. His thin brown hair is shot through with grey streaks and carefully combed. His deep brown eyes are as calm and warm as always.

'I bet you say that to all the girls,' I chuckle.

'Only you,' he vows, then reaches out to adjust my coat around the hole where my heart used to be. 'There. Perfect.' He cocks his head to examine my face.

'Burke told you what I said, didn't he?' I pout.

'Of course. If it is any help, I understand. You are not the first to stand alone, to avoid the complications of company. I went through such a spell myself. It lasted several years. I figured, if I could train myself to feel nothing for anyone, I could never be hurt again, the way I was hurt when my family was so savagely taken from me.'

'How'd you get on with that?' I ask.

'Fine,' he says. 'I found it surprisingly easy to sever all emotional ties and distance myself from those I worked with.'

'Then why did you start caring again?' I frown.

'Instinct compels many reviveds to stay with those they

knew in life,' Dr Oystein replies. 'But I do not think they truly care about those people. They have lost their souls, so they have no reason to give a damn. After a time, I realised I was behaving the same way as a revived. I came to think that God would not have restored my senses only for me to act as if I was still an unfeeling beast.

'Life was wonderful when we were alive,' the doc continues. 'We could love, procreate, bond. The downside was that we could be hurt too. But we endured the pain because the joy was so intense.

'I won't pretend that nothing has changed. We cannot love the way we once did. Everything now is a resemblance. But even a vague, loving forgery is better than experiencing only the emptiness of the damned.'

'I'm not sure I agree with you,' I say solemnly. 'It'd be different if I didn't expect to lose some of you guys any time soon. But if I was to place a bet, I wouldn't give any of you more than six months, a year tops.'

'Even though I have survived more than a hundred years already?' he asks.

'Things were different then. The world made sense. It worked. Now it's just death, destruction and loss. We're all for the chop, and I don't want to care when you, Burke or anyone else gets ripped away from us.'

'What about our response if *you* are taken?' the doctor asks quietly. 'Will you care if nobody mourns your loss, if we wipe you from our thoughts and carry on as if nothing has happened?'

'Not in the least,' I say chirpily. 'When I go, I'm gone. Makes no difference to me whether you lot celebrate or wail for a week.'

Dr Oystein nods glumly. 'As you wish. Like I said, I do understand. If you do not seek friendship, we will not force it on you. No Angel needs to care for their colleagues in order to slot in with them.

'But I do care, B, and I will continue to. Billy Burke cares about you too, and quite a few more. If you ever change your mind and crave a friend, we will be here for you. Always.'

'Unless you're killed before me,' I note.

'Touché,' he smiles. Then, smile fading, he reaches out and touches my cheek, briefly but lovingly. 'Be careful out there, B. Come home safely to us.'

He turns and leaves. I want to call him back and accept his offer of friendship, drop my guard, have at least one person in the world that I can feel close to.

But I don't.

I can't.

I won't.

I remember my friends from school. My parents. Mark. Timothy. The pain I felt at their loss. And I make a vow to myself, not for the first time since I returned to County Hall.

Never again.

SIX

We patrol the streets, entering every building we come to, checking it thoroughly. Zombies are in many of them, sheltering from the sun. We gently edge past the resting reviveds and head up flights of stairs, exploring the upper levels, looking for attics or locked doors.

We haven't found any survivors while I've been with the Angels, but lots of humans were rescued before I joined, and a few have been unearthed by other search squads since. They've had to be cunning to survive so long in a city where death is almost a certainty.

Reviveds rely heavily on their sense of smell and hearing. To outwit them, the people with the smarts douse themselves in perfume or aftershave – those smells mean nothing to a zombie, they only react to natural human scents – and wear soft shoes or slippers. The really sly ones also wrap bandages round their stomach and chest to dull the sounds of their heartbeat and digestive system, shave off their hair so they don't sweat as much and take other inventive, anti-detection measures.

The gutsier survivalists realised that once a zombie has given a building a once-over, it usually doesn't check again, unless it was accustomed to double-checking spaces when it was alive, for instance if it was a security guard. So some of the humans have made their bases in buildings which zombies frequent, the reasoning being that they're the safest places in London, since the inhabitants won't scour their own lair. Also, other reviveds recognise and respect a fellow zombie's home, and they almost never trespass. We're not sure why, it's just the way they're wired.

Angels on earlier missions to find survivors never bothered to check a building that was home to a nest of reviveds. Now, having been clued in by those we've rescued, we're more thorough.

'Oh what fun,' Rage grumbles as we exit another block of flats with nothing to show for the time spent panning around inside.

'Patience is a virtue,' Ashtat says.

'What's so special about the living anyway?' Rage sniffs. 'Why should we care about them? If they find their way to County Hall, fair enough, it would be rude not to let them in. But we could be tracking down mutants, turning the tables on hunters, kicking Mr Dowling's arse. This is a waste of our time.'

'Yeah,' Shane says, backing up his buddy as he normally does.

'Don't act like an infant,' Carl snaps. 'We're fighting this war for the sake of those who are still alive.'

'Sure,' Rage says, 'but there are millions in camps or on islands dotted around the world. What does it matter if we rustle up a few more? It's not going to make a difference.'

'It will to those we rescue,' Ashtat says.

'Well, *duh*!' Rage snorts. 'I'm talking about the bigger picture. That's what we're supposed to be looking at, right? The doc told us that the minor battles being fought across the globe are meaningless. The fight here, between us and the clown's forces, is the only real game in town. So why aren't we focusing on that? We should be too busy to play at being Good Samaritans.'

Shane nods fiercely. 'What he said.'

Ashtat and Carl scowl at Rage and Shane, but don't come back with an argument because they can't think of one. I'm not bothered. It doesn't matter to me. I just do what I'm told and try not to think too much. That should be the end of the debate, a win for Rage, but then, breaking his usual moody silence, Jakob speaks up.

'I think it's to remind us that we were once human.'

We stare at the thin, pale boy. He doesn't speak very often. It's easy to think of him as a mute.

'I forget sometimes,' he says softly. 'I find it hard to recall my life before this. It seems like I've been an undead creature for as long as I can remember.'

'So what?' Rage asks when Jakob falls silent again.

'When I feel distant from my humanity,' Jakob whispers, 'I think about linking up with Mr Dowling and his mutants. From all the reports, they have a grand time, going wherever they like, killing as they please, not caring about anyone except themselves. It must be liberating to be that brutal. The world has fallen. The walking dead have taken over. We don't neatly fit into one camp or the other. Why not throw in our lot with the clown and his crew, kill off the remaining humans and enjoy the party for the next few thousand years?'

'Blimey,' Rage laughs. 'And I thought *I* had a dark side.'

Jakob shrugs, wincing at the pain that brings to his battered, cancer-ridden body. 'That's just the way my mind wanders. Am I the only one who has thought such things?'

He looks around and everyone drops their gaze, except for Rage, who nods enthusiastically.

'Dr Oystein sees through us,' Jakob says. 'He knows all that we imagine. He can't rely on our unwavering support, because any one of us could give into desperation and temptation, and change sides.

'I think the searching, the rescues and escorting survivors to safe havens outside London are to keep us in contact with the memories of what it was like to be alive. Because if we lose those, or if they come to mean nothing to us, what's to hold us in place? Why should we bother to stay loyal?'

There's a long silence as we think about that. Jakob might not say much, but when he does speak, he tends to have something worth saying.

'Is that why you've been so distant recently?' Rage asks me. 'Are *you* thinking about stabbing us in the back and heading over Mr Dowling's way?'

'You're the only one I'd stab,' I smirk. 'I'd leave the others for the clown and his posse.'

'Then you *have* been thinking about it,' he challenges me, bristling.

'I think about all sorts of things,' I purr, baiting him, unable to resist the opportunity to get under his skin.

'If you ever –' he starts to say, raising a finger to point at me warningly.

'Rage,' Ashtat interrupts.

'Don't stick up for her,' Rage barks. 'We won't have *girl power* here. If this little –'

'Shut up,' Ashtat says calmly, 'and look to your right.'

Rage glares at her but does as she commands. I see his eyes widen, so I look too.

There are a couple of people on the street, no more than

198

ten metres ahead of us. They've come out of the remains of a shop. It's a woman and a young child. The woman is holding the child in her arms. I'm not sure if it's a boy or a girl.

But I'm sure of one thing, by the way their chests rise and fall, by the smell of the perfume they've coated themselves with, by the terror in the woman's eyes when she spots us.

They're alive.

SEVEN

For several seconds nothing happens. We stare at the woman and her child and she stares back. The child's face is turned into the woman's chest. I don't know if it's aware of us or not.

Ashtat lifts her hands over her head and calls out softly, 'We're not going to hurt you.'

The woman bolts the instant Ashtat moves. Not back into the shop, where we could trap her. Instead she turns and dashes along the street.

We start after her as a pack, acting instinctively. Carl stops us with a curt and commanding, 'Wait!'

As the rest of us pause, Carl jogs forward a couple of steps, then leaps. He lands not far behind the fleeing woman and immediately bounces into the air again, like a frog. He lands a few metres in front of her and she comes to a halt. Turns frantically, looking for an escape route. She spots an open door in a building and starts towards it.

'That's not a wise move,' Carl says calmly. 'There could be a dozen zombies on the other side of that door.'

The woman stops and stares at Carl. Then looks back at the rest of us. We're all standing still.

'What are you?' the woman gasps, taking another step away from Carl, edging closer to the door, caught in two minds.

'That's a long story,' Carl chuckles. 'All you need to know right now is that we mean you no harm. We're not going to attack you. We won't even detain you. If you're suspicious of us and don't want to talk, you can carry on down this street and we won't lift a finger to stop you. I'll just say two words to you before you go. *County Hall.*'

Carl shuffles out into the middle of the road. The woman licks her lips nervously, then starts to run. She thinks this is a trick. I don't blame her.

Nobody moves, even though we'll all hate it if we lose her. I say a silent prayer that she'll stop and look back. But then she turns a corner and disappears from sight. I feel my spirits sinking. I look around and everyone is staring glumly at the spot where she vanished, even Rage.

'Hard luck, Carl,' Ashtat says. 'At least you tried. I thought –'

'Wait a minute,' Carl hushes her. He's smiling hopefully.

The fingers of his left hand are flexing slowly, as if trying to beckon the woman back. I don't think there's any chance of that, but I hold my peace along with the other Angels. I count inside my head, determined to give Carl the full minute he asked for. After that, I'll tell him to forget it, we can't win them all, maybe next time luck will be on our . . .

The woman edges back into view. First it's just her head, as she stares at us. Then she steps on to our street. She's still holding the child. It's looking at us now and I see that's it's a boy. Just four or five years old, but well drilled, silent as a butterfly.

The woman slips closer, studying the houses on either side, eyeing us uneasily. She stops a good distance away from Carl. She's trembling.

'You could have leapt through the air again and stopped me,' she says.

Carl nods.

'Why didn't you?'

'We don't want to trap you,' Carl says. 'If I tried to get in your way, you might run into me and scratch yourself. That would be bad.'

'Then you *are* a zombie?'

'A certain kind, yes.'

'Not the kind that eats brains?'

Carl laughs softly. 'Oh, we definitely eat brains, we have to. But we don't take them from the living. And we don't kill. We're your friendly neighbourhood kind of zombie.'

The woman doesn't smile but she stops shaking so much. 'And County Hall?' she asks. 'What did you mean?'

'It's where we're based,' Carl explains. 'If you don't want to come with us, that's cool, we won't force you. But if you're ever in need of allies or shelter, or looking for a way out of the city, come to County Hall and we'll help. You'll be safe there. It's the safest place in London.'

'Nowhere's truly safe,' the woman says.

'Not truly,' Carl concedes. 'But if you seek refuge there, and anyone wants to do you harm, they'll have to cut through us first.'

'What are you?' the woman asks again, frowning now.

'Like I said, that's a long story. But if you want to know *who* we are, I'm Carl Clay and these guys will be more than happy to introduce themselves if you let them.'

The woman wavers, takes a step back, thinks about it some more, then makes up her mind. 'I'm Emma,' she says. 'This is my son, Declan.'

'A pleasure to meet you, Emma,' Carl says, smiling broadly. 'Now, do you know any place around here where we could get a decent cup of coffee?'

And when he says that, despite herself, Emma returns the smile, and as sappy as it might sound, it's one of the most heart-warming things I've ever seen. Even for an undead, heart-deprived monster like me.

EIGHT

Carl wasn't joking about the coffee. He tells us that one of his uncles ran a small espresso bar in Kensington. Carl used to work there occasionally at the weekends, learning the trade. His parents thought it would be good for him, help keep his feet on the ground—he comes from a wealthy background and I guess they didn't want him losing touch with us common folk.

We find a deserted café, Carl takes Emma's order and heads in, delighted with himself. The rest of us wait on the street. Emma stands apart from us, still unsure she made the right choice when she came back. Declan is ogling us. He seems particularly fascinated by the hole in my chest.

'I'd let you poke about in there,' I smile at him, 'but it's dangerous.'

Declan blushes and hides his face. Emma laughs and rubs his head. 'No need to be afraid,' she coos. 'These people aren't going to hurt us. He was always shy,' she tells me. 'I used to encourage him to be more outgoing, but in this climate shyness isn't a bad thing. I haven't had any trouble keeping him quiet.'

I nod understandingly. 'Noise attracts the zombies.'

'Smells attract them too,' Ashtat mutters, looking around, worried. 'If any nearby reviveds get a whiff of that coffee …'

'Don't brick it,' Rage laughs. 'We can handle a few dumb reviveds if we have to.'

'But I'd rather not risk it,' Ashtat says and goes to see how Carl is getting on.

'Do other zombies attack you?' Emma asks me.

'Not usually,' I reply. 'But if we got in the way of a feed, they would.'

'Then we're putting you in danger.'

I shrug. 'We don't mind a little danger. It's what we're here for.'

Carl emerges with a mug of steaming hot coffee, beaming as if he'd delivered a newborn baby. Emma thanks him and reaches for it.

'Uh-uh,' he stops her and carefully lays the mug down on the ground for her to pick up. 'Best not to take any chances.'

'This is so weird,' she says, pulling a face as she retrieves the mug. 'If anyone had told me this morning that a zombie would be serving me coffee before the day was out …'

We all laugh, but quietly, so as not to draw attention. Then we head for Leicester Square, talking softly as we progress. We tell Emma about ourselves, how we differ from reviveds, the way we try to help living survivors, Dr Oystein and the set-up at County Hall. By the time we get to the small park at the heart of the West End and make ourselves comfy on a few of the benches, Emma is shaking her head with wonder.

'I never would have dreamt this was possible. I thought you were all killers.'

'Most of us are,' Ashtat says. 'Do not make the mistake of thinking you should give zombies a chance from now on. If you ever see one coming towards you, run. There are very few of our type around.'

'What about you guys?' Shane asks. 'How did you survive this long?'

'By being very careful,' Emma sighs. 'And with a lot of luck.'

'Are there more of you?' Carl asks. 'Do you want us to fetch the others and take them back to County Hall? Assuming you want to go there,' he adds quickly. 'No pressure. We'll understand if you'd rather stick to what you know.'

'Are you kidding?' Emma says bitterly. 'I hate what we've had to endure, the places we've had to stay, the loneliness. Of course we're coming with you. If I'd only known about you before ...'

She starts to cry. The rest of us say nothing and look away awkwardly, waiting for the tears to pass. Declan makes a small whining sound and, when I glance at him, I see him stroking his mother's hair and kissing her cheek. I recall the monstrous babies from my dreams, and the all-too-real baby at Timothy's, and suppress a shudder.

'Sorry,' Emma moans when the tears finally pass. 'I've been holding those in for so long. I didn't want to cry before this. I was afraid I might not be able to stop once I'd started, that I might start howling with grief and rage.'

'Howling's not good in this city,' Shane notes. 'It draws a crowd.'

'Yes.' Emma wipes tears away and grins at us, embarrassed. 'Sorry,' she says again.

'No need to apologise,' Ashtat smiles. 'We would love to cry if we could.'

Emma blinks. 'You mean you can't?'

'Unfortunately not. We are, in most respects, dead. There are many things the undead can no longer do—cry, sweat, breathe.'

Emma shakes her head, amazed, and drains the last of her coffee. 'That was so good,' she says.

'I can make you some more if you'd like,' Carl offers.

'Not right now,' she says. 'Maybe in a while. I don't like to drink too much. I'm always afraid the smell might tip off the zombies. Does it?'

'I'm not sure,' Carl says. 'Most reviveds aren't good at association. That's why they don't link the smell of perfume or aftershave to the living. But I've seen some react to the scent of food before. I think they remember that only a living human would bother with food, since the walking dead don't eat. Well, except for brains obviously.'

'But you're safe with us,' Shane brags. 'You can have a barbecue if you like, here in the Square. We'll run off any nosy buggers who come sniffing round.'

Emma giggles. 'A barbecue! This is like a dream. I wish . . .' She pauses and her expression darkens. 'I wish Shaun could have been here. He practically lived for bar-becues. He was Australian. He grew up cooking outdoors.'

'Was Shaun your husband?' Ashtat asks delicately.

'No,' Emma grunts. '*He* left the picture long before the zombies struck, and good riddance to him. I hope he was one of the first to die and that it was painful and slow.' She glowers, then chuckles. 'I don't mean that really. But I cer-tainly wouldn't shed any tears if I found out he was dead.

'Shaun was a friend of mine. We were together the day the zombies took over. He was a survival expert, he loved challenging himself in harsh terrains, he'd spend his holi-days cheating death in hellholes around the world. I thought he was crazy, but he used to say a beach holiday was his idea of purgatory. He wasn't happy when he went away unless he staggered back bloody, bruised and exhausted.

'I was glad of his skills after the attacks,' she goes on. 'We wouldn't have lasted long without him. He taught us how to hide and forage. He studied the zombies, learnt about them, helped us stay one step ahead. I wanted to flee the city, but Shaun said we stood a better chance here, at least to begin with. I kept urging him to take us to one of the settlements in the countryside, or to try for an island, but he was sceptical. He didn't believe all of the reports on the radio. He wanted to let things settle. I also think he was reluctant to put his life in the hands of anyone else. He liked his independence.'

'Did the zombies get him?' I ask.

Emma nods. 'We picked up other survivors along the way. We numbered eight at our maximum. Shaun always told me not to let myself get too attached to them. He said if we ever got backed into a corner, we had to abandon the others and look after ourselves. He said we couldn't afford the luxury of friends any more.'

'Sounds like he knew what he was doing,' I mutter, thinking about my talk with Mr Burke.

'Yes,' Emma sighs. 'But he couldn't follow his own advice in the end. We lost a couple of members to attacks over the months. Another couple struck out for the countryside by themselves. A few more joined up. Shaun was always in command. He was a natural leader. Nobody in the group ever challenged him.

'One of the new guys was diabetic. He needed insulin. We were in a chemist's. Zombies were nesting on the upper floor. They chased us. The guy with diabetes got trapped. Shaun went back for him. He shouldn't have. If I'd done it, he would have bawled me out. But you could never tell Shaun anything.'

Emma starts weeping again but softly this time. 'That was a couple of months ago. Those of us who were left stayed together for a few weeks. Then the others decided to leave London. I hung on, remembering what Shaun had said. We've been alone since then, haven't we, Declan?'

The little boy nods stiffly. He's crying too now, but quietly, shivering in his mother's arms.

'You've done well to survive,' Jakob says softly. 'Shaun would be proud.'

Emma nods and sniffs. Carl chews on his lower lip, wanting to say something more to comfort the pair. Then he has a brainwave.

'Does Declan have any toys?' he asks.

Both Emma and Declan stop crying and stare at Carl. 'No,' Emma says. 'I pick up some things for him every now and then, if we're staying in one spot for a few nights, but we move around a lot and we can't carry much with us when we travel. Toys are pretty low on our list of priorities.'

'I figured as much,' Carl says, getting to his feet. 'We're not that far from Hamleys. Why don't I pop over there and find some really cool toys for him to play with in County Hall?'

'I'm not sure,' Emma says. 'I've passed by Hamleys a few times. It's full of zombies. I never dared go in.'

'They won't bother *me*,' Carl laughs and sets off, excited at the thought of exploring the different levels of the famous old toyshop.

'Do you want us to come with you?' Ashtat asks.

'No,' he says. 'Stay here and enjoy the sun. Emma and Declan will be safer in the open, with plenty of escape routes.'

'Hold on,' I stop him. 'I'm coming.'

'I don't need back-up,' he snorts.

'I'm sure you don't. Still, it can't hurt having someone to look out for you. And I can give you a hand bringing stuff back.'

Carl thinks about that and shrugs. 'OK, if you want. Just as long as we're clear that I'm the one who gets to choose.'

'Don't worry about it,' I say drily. 'I know better than to come between a boy and his toys.'

Carl starts to retort, then remembers that there's a young child present. He catches himself, grins sheepishly at Emma, then off we head in search of some toys that will hopefully bring a smile to the solemn boy's face.

NINE

'You didn't need to tag along,' Carl says as we exit the Square and head towards Regent Street.

'You shouldn't go off solo,' I grunt. 'Anything could happen to you.'

'Would you be bothered?' Carl asks.

I shrug. 'I don't want to have to explain your loss to Master Zhang.'

Carl smiles. '*You* went off by yourself after you fell from the London Eye.'

I haven't told them that Rage pushed me. They think I fell. I didn't even tell Dr Oystein. I'm not a tattletale. What happened on the Eye was between Rage and me.

'I'm a special case,' I mutter.

Carl looks at me sideways and smirks. 'I think you fancy me.'

'In your dreams.'

'That's why you've come. You can't bear to be parted from me.'

I fake a yawn. 'Yeah, that's it.' Then I tell him, 'Actually it's because of the book.'

He frowns. 'What are you talking about?'

'The book with the Van Gogh letters. It's great. You gave it to me, so I wanted to repay you.'

'It's no big deal,' he says. 'You could have given me a book in return.'

'I couldn't be arsed looking for one.'

He grins. 'Or you could have just said thanks.'

'Nothing says thank you better than saving a person's life,' I drawl.

Carl shakes his head. 'You're a strange one, Smith.'

'Am I?'

'Yes. I can't figure you out. I try being nice to you, and you clearly appreciate that or you wouldn't feel compelled to repay me. But instead of just accepting me as a friend, you have to turn it into something weird.'

'Nothing weird about it,' I grunt. 'I liked the book. This is my way of doing something nice for you in return.'

'You could simply be my friend,' Carl says.

'I'd rather save your neck.'

'Even though you don't like me?' he presses.

'I never said I didn't like you.'

'Then you do like me?'

213

'I never said that either.'

Carl stops and squints. 'Are you playing mind games with me?'

'No.' I roll my eyes. 'You're just a guy I work with, same as the others. I'm happy to keep things pleasant, but I don't want to do more than that. Friends aren't my thing.'

'Must be lonely up there in that tower,' Carl says.

'Suits me fine,' I retort. 'Now, are we sorting out those toys or what?'

Carl looks at me a beat longer, then shrugs and starts off again. He doesn't say anything else. I don't either. I didn't want to piss him off, but he kept asking until there was nothing else for it but to hit him with the truth.

After a short, uneventful journey, we stop outside Hamleys. Any time I passed by before, it was swarming with kids and tourists. Now it's no different to any other large building in this city, silent, no signs of life, just the occasional flickering shadow as zombies shift around inside.

'It's sad,' Carl says. 'It feels more like a graveyard than a toyshop now.'

'Do you want to try somewhere else?' I ask.

'No. The other places will be the same. I'll go look inside, see what I can rustle up. I might be a while—I always seem to turn into a big kid in here. Do you want to come with me, or do you want to browse by yourself?'

'Actually I think I'll stay out here and keep watch,' I say, not wanting to go in and be confronted with all those toys, along with the realisation that no children will ever come to play with them again. 'I'll give you a shout if I spot anything.'

'Like what?' he laughs. 'Elephants?'

'Just get on with your job, *toy boy*,' I growl and move away from the door, out of his line of sight.

As Carl goes on the hunt for the perfect present, I shuffle along, away from the windows which are still packed with displays of toys that haven't been disturbed, until I come to a stretch of wall that I can lean against. I glance around idly, then study my fingerbones, picking at them, cleaning them. I keep them in good shape, but with all the training and fighting, they get scraped and chipped. The scuffs don't really bother me, but I like to keep them neat and tidy. I guess filing down the bones is the closest I get to polishing my nails these days.

As I'm digging at a thin crack in one of the bones, trying to scrape out the dirt, I hear something rustling to my left. I look up but can't see anything. Probably just a rat. I return my attention to my bones, but then there's a shuffling sound off to my right. I frown and step away from the wall, squinting. The sun's in my eyes. I raise a hand to shade them.

Something strikes the back of my neck and a surge of electricity crackles through me. Every muscle in my body goes haywire. I collapse instantly. I try to cry out with pain, but my mouth won't work. It's like I'm filling with sparks. Lights dance across my eyes and I go temporarily blind.

As my vision starts to clear, a man rushes towards me. A gag is shoved into my mouth. My hands are jerked behind my back and tied together. Someone else binds my legs. I want to scream for help, but I'm still spasming and the gag would stop me making any noises anyway.

The guy who bound my hands starts to jam a thick sack down over my head. He pauses before he covers my eyes and waits for me to focus on him. As I do, the world swimming slowly back into place around me, I spot his dark, grey-streaked hair and brown eyes, and I think it's Dr Oystein, that this is a test.

Then the man's features solidify and I realise it's not the doc. I don't know why I ever thought it was. The pair look nothing alike. This guy is much broader, with a menacing expression, and Dr Oystein never went around with a bullet stuck behind his right ear.

When I spot the bullet, everything clicks and I realise what's going on. I try to scream again, to at least alert Carl, even if it's too late for me. But the hunter knows his job. He's not in the habit of making mistakes.

'Hello again, my bizarre little beauty,' he whispers.

And, as he tugs the sack down over my face, thrusting me into darkness, I try screaming one last time, unsuccessfully willing myself to bellow his name out loud for all the world to hear.

'*Barnes!*'

TEN

My captors pick me up and hurry along the street with me. I try kicking out at them, but I'm expertly bound and my muscles are still throbbing from the shock. I've never been tasered before. I didn't think it would hurt so much. My head is ringing and it feels like I've been sucking batteries for a week.

I'm bundled into the back of a van and the doors slam shut. The engine starts and we lurch forward. It's been so long since I was in a moving vehicle, the sensation is strange. I get a bit nauseous. I never suffered from travel sickness when I was alive. Maybe it has something to do with my altered hearing.

I've no idea what's going on. Barnes is a hunter. When I met him before, he was leading a small team, killing zombies for sport. I could understand that. But why kidnap me now instead of shoot me dead when he had the chance? Does he plan to torture me?

I wouldn't have thought he was the type. That day in the East End, when he realised I could think and speak, he let me go. He even threatened to eliminate one of his crew, Coley, a nasty piece of work who wanted to kill me despite the fact I wasn't like the other zombies.

But maybe I caught Barnes on a soft day. He might have thought about it since then and decided I was fair game. Perhaps he got tired of executing mindless zombies and wanted to experiment on one who could react to his taunts.

As I'm considering the nature of the man who now controls my fate, the sack is pulled free of my head. Barnes is squatting in front of me, grinning bleakly.

'I know you haven't forgotten me,' he says quietly in his American accent. 'You're in trouble and I won't pretend you're not. But I'm not figuring on killing you. If you play ball, you might get out of this alive. Now, do you want me to take out that gag?'

I nod sharply.

'If you try to bite me, I'll execute you,' he says, showing me a hunting knife. 'I'll dig this straight into your brain at the first snap of your teeth.'

I glare at Barnes as he reaches out and removes the gag, but slide my head backwards as soon as my mouth is free, away from his gloved fingers, to signal to him that I'm not going to strike. Barnes didn't bother with gloves the first time I met him, but I guess he's racked up the stakes a level and is getting much closer to zombies now. If you're gonna get hands-on with one of us, you need to be more cautious.

'How did you find me?' I snarl.

'I've been staking out Leicester Square and the area around it for several weeks,' he says. 'I guessed you – or those like you – would swing through sooner or later. The Square might have fallen from grace, but it's still the heart of the city.

'I've seen you before,' he continues. 'A few times. But you were always part of a group. I didn't want to target you when you were with company. Too complicated. Always easier to pick off a stray.

'Actually I wasn't after you specifically,' he adds. 'Any one of you would have done. But I had a feeling it would be you. The universe works strangely that way. I don't believe in destiny, but coincidence is a far more complex beast than most people give it credit for.'

'God bless coincidence,' the driver laughs. 'I'm glad you didn't let me kill her all those months ago.'

'Coley?' I growl. Barnes's hunting partner wanted to shoot me when our paths first crossed. Barnes wouldn't let him. Rather, he said he'd let Coley shoot me, but that he'd disable him in return and leave him for the zombies as punishment.

'Guess you didn't think you'd be seeing me again,' Coley snickers.

'Not this side of Hell,' I snarl. 'I hoped a zombie would have ripped you apart by now.'

'Not this fleet-footed fox,' Coley boasts.

'I'm surprised you're still together,' I mutter. 'I thought you'd have gone your separate ways after what happened, Barnes threatening to shoot off your kneecaps and all.'

'Nothing more than a minor quarrel,' Coley says, glancing over his shoulder to show me his grin. He's sporting fancy designer glasses, the same as before. His straw-coloured hair is a bit longer. Both men are wearing army fatigues.

'A lovers' tiff?' I murmur, smiling back at Coley as best I can from my awkward position.

Coley's face darkens. 'I say we cut out her tongue.'

Barnes chuckles. 'Not yet. Our lords and ladies might want her to sing for them first.'

'What's going on?' I ask.

'You'll find out soon,' Barnes tells me.

'You won't like it when you do,' Coley cackles and takes a bend sharply, tyres squealing. Barnes almost topples on to me.

'Careful!' he barks.

'Don't worry,' Coley says. 'I'm in total control of this baby.' We hit a bump and Barnes is jolted into the air. Again he has to steady himself before he falls within range of my infectious teeth.

'I won't warn you again,' Barnes says.

'You're no fun,' Coley pouts but slows to a more reasonable speed.

Barnes scowls at the back of his partner's head, then leans in close to me. 'If it's any consolation,' he whispers so that only I can hear, 'I hate having to do this. It won't mean much to you, I know, but for what it's worth, I'm sorry.'

And the sad look he flashes me is far more worrying than any threat he might have made.

ELEVEN

We drive for what feels like twenty or thirty minutes. It involves a lot of zigzagging around crashed or abandoned vehicles, which slows us down. A few zombies hurl themselves at the vehicle every now and then, but they bounce off and are easily left behind. Coley swerves on other occasions to deliberately mow down zombies that are in his path. He whoops every time he hits one, sometimes pausing to reverse over them, trying to squash their heads.

Barnes sighs and purses his lips with disapproval, but says nothing, letting Coley have his grisly fun.

The van finally draws to a halt and Coley kills the engine. Having checked the mirrors to make sure the area is clear of the living dead, he hops out, trots round to the back and opens the doors. 'Here, kitty, kitty,' he purrs and reaches in for me. He grabs my feet and starts to pull me out.

'Wait until I gag her,' Barnes says.

'Don't,' I ask him as he leans towards me. 'I won't bite, I swear.'

'I believe you but I can't take any chances,' he says. 'It won't be for long, just until we can set you down.'

Barnes puts the gag back in place and secures it. Then he nods at Coley, who happily hauls me out of the van. I land on the ground with a thump. Coley kicks me while I'm down, hard in the ribs.

'Not such a tough girl now, are you?' he spits.

'There's no need for that,' Barnes says wearily, climbing out of the van and shutting the doors.

'Don't tell me you're going to shoot me just for kicking her,' Coley giggles.

Barnes frowns. 'Some days I wonder why I keep you around.'

'Because I'm good at what I do,' Coley says smugly, kicking me again. 'It's the same reason I put up with your righteous crap. We work well together. We need each other, much as it might pain either of us to admit it.'

Barnes cracks his knuckles and casts an eye over me. 'You take the legs,' he says. 'I'll take the upper body.'

'You sure?' Coley asks.

'Yeah. You'd keep dropping her on her head otherwise.'

Coley laughs with delight then picks up my legs. Barnes slips his hands under my shoulders and lifts. They juggle me around until they're comfortable, then start ahead. They're both strong men and they might as well be carrying a small dog for all the effort it takes them. Even so, I'm guessing they won't want to carry me too far – they're vulnerable with me in their hands, easy prey if zombies attack – and I'm proved right a minute later when they pass by the cool glass building of City Hall, head down to the bank of the Thames and take a left.

HMS *Belfast* is docked ahead of us. I came this way when I first trekked across from the east. There were people on the deck of the famous old cruiser, armed to the teeth. They shot at me before I could ask any questions, scared me off, made it clear they didn't welcome strangers. They're still up there and look to be just as heavily armed. But they don't fire at Barnes and Coley. It seems like they're expecting us.

The hunters carry me up the gangway. They don't say anything. Once onboard, they lay me down and take a step back. The people with the rifles press closer. There are at least a dozen of them, more spread across the deck. They look like soldiers although they're dressed in suits. They don't smile, just stare at me with distaste.

'Is this one of the speaking zombies?' a man in a suit and wearing shades like Coley's asks.

'Yeah,' Barnes replies.

'You finally came good and caught one,' the man sniffs.

'I swore that I would.'

'Took you long enough.'

Barnes smiles tightly. 'If you thought you could do better, you should have said so. I'd have been happy to spend my days lounging around here and let you go scour the streets instead.'

The man in the suit scowls. 'Think you're hot stuff, don't you, Barnes?'

Barnes shrugs. 'I'm just a guy who gets the job done. Now, are the lords and ladies of the Board ready to accept their delivery?'

'Wait here,' the man says. 'I'll go check.'

There's a short delay. Barnes and Coley stand at ease. The people with the rifles keep them trained on me, ready to blast me to hell if I show the slightest sign that I'm about to try to break free.

Eventually someone comes running towards us. 'Let me see! Let me see!' a panting man cries and the guards around us part.

I spot a fat man in a sailor suit prancing across the deck. The suit is too small for him and his stomach is exposed. It's hairy and there are crumbs stuck in the hairs.

The fat man crouches next to me and stares, eyes wide, lips quivering. He notes the hole in my chest and studies my face. His smile fades. 'It's a girl. I thought it would be a boy.'

'I didn't know you had a preference,' Barnes says. 'Does it make any difference?'

The fat man purses his lips. 'I suppose not. I just

assumed . . .' He shrugs and smiles again. 'Make her talk, Barnes. Make her talk for Dan-Dan. I want to hear her before the others. I want to be the first.'

Barnes looks at the guard in the suit and glasses, who has followed behind the guy dressed like a sailor. The guard shrugs. Barnes carefully removes my gag and shifts out of my way.

The fat man nods at me, grinning like a lunatic. 'Come on, little girl. Talk for Dan-Dan. Let me hear you.'

I look *Dan-Dan* up and down, slow as you like, then smile lazily. 'You're about three sizes too large for that ridiculous suit, fat boy.'

Dan-Dan's jaw drops. Some of the guards smirk. Coley snorts with laughter. Barnes just stares at me.

'You . . . you . . .' Dan-Dan sputters. He starts to swing a hand at me, to slap me. Then he remembers what I am and stops. His smile swims back into place and he blows me a kiss. 'You're wonderful,' he gurgles. 'A spirited, snarling, she-snake. Everything I was hoping for and more. We're going to have so much fun with you, little girl.'

Dan-Dan lurches to his feet and claps his hands at Barnes and Coley. 'Don't stand there like fools,' he barks, going from buffoon to commander in the space of a few seconds. 'Bring her through to the Wardroom. The others are waiting and we're not renowned for our patience.'

As Barnes and Coley pick me up again – pausing only to

stick my gag back in place – Dan-Dan sets off ahead of us. He waddles like a duck but there's nothing funny about him now. I'm in serious trouble here. And while the farcically dressed fat man is nowhere near as scary as Mr Dowling or Owl Man, he's probably more of a threat than either of them. Both of those freaks chose to let me run free, but I've a horrible feeling that Dan-Dan wants me for keeps.

TWELVE

Barnes and Coley carry me across the deck, down a flight of stairs, then towards the rear of the cruiser, which they refer to as the aft. Dan-Dan trots ahead of us, skipping at times, singing to himself.

Dan-Dan opens a door and we enter a long room dominated by a massive table. It could easily seat a couple of dozen people, but only five individuals are sitting around it. They're spread out, as if they don't want to sit too close to one another. There are ten guards in the room, standing by the walls, surrounding the table. All have handguns and are pointing them at me.

Coley chuckles uneasily. 'You guys want to lower those? If you fire off a shot accidentally, you might hit Barnes or me.'

'There will be no accidents here,' a woman at the table says. She's in her forties or fifties. Dressed to the nines, dripping in necklaces and diamonds. If she looked any posher, she'd be a queen.

Dan-Dan takes a seat and chortles. 'Lady Jemima is correct, as always. If we shoot you, it will be on purpose.'

Barnes ignores the veiled threat and helps Coley set me on my feet. 'Her name's Becky Smith,' he tells the six people at the table. 'She's one of the talking zombies.'

'It's true,' Dan-Dan gushes. 'I heard her speak on deck. She insulted me. I didn't like that—she's a naughty little minx who must be taught the error of her ways. But she can definitely speak.'

'We never doubted you, Barnes,' another man says. He's smartly dressed in a purple suit. He looks young, but there are faint wrinkles around his eyes when he smiles, which make me think he's older than he appears. 'We were just concerned that it was taking you so long to find one for us.'

Barnes shuffles his feet and pulls a face. 'I'm slow but sure.' It's an act. There's nothing slow about Barnes. But he's clearly wary of these people and their armed guards.

'Remove the gag,' one of the other men says. This one has an eastern European accent. He's dressed like a prince, crown and all.

'Yes, sir,' Barnes murmurs and reaches up to free my mouth. 'Be careful what you say to them,' he whispers. 'They don't have a sense of humour.'

I stare silently at my regally attired captors when the gag has been removed.

'Well?' Lady Jemima asks, twisting a diamond ring as she bores into me with her gaze.

'What?' I sniff and she stops turning the ring.

'Incredible,' she sighs.

'She spoke to me first,' Dan-Dan crows. 'Did you hear that, Luca?' he calls to the guy in the purple suit. 'I was first.'

'Mother would be so proud of you,' Luca purrs sarcastically. 'If you hadn't thrown her to a zombie to save yourself, that is.'

Dan-Dan's face drops. 'I thought we weren't going to mention that again.'

Luca sniffs and leans towards me. 'Tell us about yourself, girl. Where are you from? How can you speak? Are there many more like you?'

I cock my head at him and don't answer. He studies me silently, then grins viciously. 'The next time you refuse to answer a question, I'll have one of my men cut off the little finger on your left hand. After that, it will be your head. I only believe in a single warning. So, unless you're keen to die today, talk.'

'There's not much I can tell you,' I say sullenly. 'I don't know how I can talk or why I'm different.' That's a lie, but I'm not going to rat out Dr Oystein to this pack of creeps.

I think about saying I'm a one-off, but Barnes has seen me with other Angels. I have to be careful, lie cautiously, mix in a bit of truth.

'There are several of us that I know about. We wander around London together. We've been looking for answers but haven't found any, so we've been getting by as best we can.'

'Does the girl need to eat brains?' the other woman at the table asks. She's conservatively dressed in a dark jacket and trousers. Grey hair. A pinched face. 'Ask her if she needs to eat brains, Luca.'

'Ask her yourself,' Luca snaps.

The woman frowns. 'I don't want to talk to one of *them*. She's a thing, not a person.'

'But you're happy for me to talk to her?' Luca growls.

'You're more natural in situations like this,' the woman simpers.

Luca barks a laugh. 'You're useless, Vicky. I don't know how you got into Parliament so many times.'

'By being ruthless with people who displease me,' Vicky says flatly.

'Peace,' the final man to speak says. He's the oldest, a white-haired, thick-limbed guy. The others quit squabbling immediately. The man rises and crosses the room to study me up close. If I leant forward quickly, I could bite him. But it would be my final act and he knows it. I don't smell any fear on him.

'My name is Justin Bazini,' he says. 'If you had the right connections, you would know what that name means. I'm a man of immense wealth and power. Those are Lords Luca and Daniel Wood, not as well off as my good self, but not short of a few shillings either.'

'What are shillings?' Dan-Dan asks jokingly.

Justin points at the overdressed woman. 'Lady Jemima. You probably saw her picture a lot in the fashion magazines when you were alive.'

'I didn't waste my time reading fashion mags,' I sniff.

He looks down at my clothes and smiles mockingly. 'Evidently not. Our other good lady is Victoria Wedge. I imagine you weren't the most political of creatures, so I don't suppose you –'

'I know who Vicky Wedge is,' I interrupt. 'I don't recognise the face but I know the name. My dad used to talk about her. He thought the sun shone out of her backside. Not too fond of foreigners, was she?'

'There is nothing wrong with foreigners,' Vicky Wedge says with an icy smile. 'As long as they are invited foreigners who can be of benefit to their adopted homeland. Was your father one of my supporters?'

'Yeah. He had the real hots for you. He always had a soft spot for bigots.'

I expect her to flush at the insult but she only laughs. 'What a charmless little beast. The perfect example of why

I campaigned for chemical castration of the more vulgar, useless proletariat.'

'You surely did not campaign openly about such a controversial issue, did you?' the guy with the crown asks.

'No,' Vicky scowls. 'My spin doctors advised against it. They thought it might inspire some of the vile creatures to crawl to the polling stations to vote against me.'

'And, finally, the gentleman with the crown is The Prince.' Justin wraps up the introductions.

'No actual name?' I ask.

'I prefer not to use it,' The Prince says grandly. 'In this world I am one of the last of my kind. One day I will be *the* last. People might as well get used to calling me by my title.'

'Not interested in being king?' I sneer.

'Oh no,' The Prince says. 'Nobody likes a king. But everyone loves a prince. I want to be loved. I *will* be loved.'

Justin returns to his seat and rocks back and forth as he addresses me. 'We are the Board. We happened to be together here in London when the world fell. Rather than flee, as so many in our position did, we stood firm and made this vessel our own, choosing it both because it's easier to defend than a landlocked building and because it's such a potent reminder of our glorious past.'

'Plus I've always liked big boats,' Dan-Dan giggles. 'Sailors are my favourite military personnel. Their uniforms are to die for.'

'We're going to run this world again one day,' Luca says.

'And run it the right way this time,' Vicky Wedge adds pointedly.

'From here?' I ask sceptically.

'Of course not,' Justin snaps. 'This is merely a temporary base. But we will maintain our position in London, you can be sure of that. Once the situation has stabilised and we've rid the streets of their zombie scum, we'll recover Downing Street and Buckingham Palace, and run the world from the heart of the great British Empire, as it always should have been.'

'*Rule Britannia*,' Dan-Dan sings at the top of his voice.

'I think the army might have something to say about that,' I mutter.

'Nonsense,' The Prince chuckles. 'Soldiers exist to be given orders. No military junta ever ruled for long. They will need leaders to guide them.'

'And you think you guys fit the bill?'

'Who else?' Justin challenges me. 'The other survivors of our stature, who might have provided competition, fled like frightened animals when the chips were down. Class will always triumph. We stood firm and that will be acknowledged.'

'You're cuckoo,' I sniff, ignoring Barnes's warning to be careful about what I say. 'Money doesn't matter any more. You won't be able to buy your way into power again.'

'Foolish child,' Lady Jemima laughs.

'Ignorant brat,' Vicky Wedge adds snidely.

'Money will always be a factor,' Dan-Dan says, dropping the man-child act. 'Cash might not be worth what it was, but diamonds and gold hold their value no matter what.'

'We have plenty of those stored away,' Luca boasts.

'And we know where we can get more,' The Prince beams, rubbing his hands together greedily.

'In short,' Justin concludes, 'we're perfectly positioned to take control of the world. It will happen, there is no question of that. It's just a matter of when. And until then we're keen to kill time.' He's been drumming his fingers on the table. Now he stops and points at me. 'That's where *you* come in. Tell me, Miss Smith, do you have a taste for combat? If you don't,' he adds quickly before I can answer, 'fret not, dear girl, because you will develop one soon, once the killing begins . . .'

THIRTEEN

The members of the Board file out of the Wardroom, Dan-Dan moving swiftly to make sure he's at the head of the procession. Half the guards go with them. The other half keep their weapons trained on me.

'What's going on here?' I ask Barnes.

He doesn't answer. Instead it's Coley who says, 'Entertainment will always be a thriving industry. Our lords and ladies wish to be amused, and they have the funds in place to ensure those wishes are met.'

'You can't care about money now,' I mutter, again addressing my comments to Barnes. 'Those power-hungry leeches are doolally. We can never go back to the old ways.'

'I'm not too sure about that,' Barnes says softly. 'But no, I'm not in it for the money.'

'Then what?' I growl. 'The kicks? Do you like seeing zombies suffer?'

Barnes only stares at me.

'He has his reasons,' Coley says defensively.

'And they're mine to share or not,' Barnes barks.

'Easy, big guy,' Coley chuckles. 'I wasn't going to say any more.'

'What about you?' I sniff.

'I like the work and I like the perks,' Coley grins. 'There are women here who look kindly on brave soldiers like me. We have access to alcohol, drugs, anything we want. Power and wealth mean nothing to me. It's all about the fringe benefits.'

A guard comes to fetch us and leads us to an even larger, longer room. Some poles run along the middle, supporting the ceiling. Thick glass panels have been set in place along one side of the room, the side with small round windows in it. Panels also cover the far end of the room, where there's an access door. The result is a sealed, self-contained, L-shaped corridor.

The half-dozen members of the Board are standing on the other side of the glass, in the corridor. The Prince and Justin Bazini are puffing fat cigars. Lady Jemima is smoking a cigarette clasped in a long, fancy holder. Lord Luca pops a few pills. Vicky Wedge is leaning against the glass, breathing heavily, her arms crossed, and Dan-Dan is close by her, tapping on the glass with his fingers, cooing at me as if I was a caged bird. At one point he leans forward and licks the glass. Then he draws a little heart in his spit and flutters his eyelashes at me.

There are bloodstains smeared across the glass on my side. Bits of flesh are stuck to it in places. Bones are scattered across the floor.

'Can you hear us, little girl?' Dan-Dan calls. 'Is the sound system working? It had better be. I don't like it when that breaks down. Heads will roll if there are any technical problems today.'

'We can hear you loud and clear, Lord Wood,' Coley replies.

Dan-Dan smiles. 'I can hear you too. That's perfect.'

'Unbind her and come on round,' Justin says to Barnes and Coley. 'We want to share the show with you, a reward for all the hard work you've put in over the last few weeks.'

Barnes faces me. 'We can do this the hard way if you want. I can taser you and release you while you're subdued. But if you give me your word not to attack us, we can just take off the cuffs and leave you be.'

'No need for the taser,' I beam. 'I'll be a good girl. Promise.'

Barnes stares at me for a few beats, then grins tightly. 'I don't believe you.'

I drop the fake smile. 'That's because I'm lying. If I get the chance, I'll rip your throats open and wallow in your blood before you die.'

'You'd rather the taser?'

'Bring it on.'

Barnes sighs and gives Coley the nod. 'I'm loving this,' Coley says, then lets me have it. I collapse in a spasming heap. Stars fill my head again. The agony is even worse than the first time and seems to last longer.

As I start to recover, I realise that my hands and legs are free. Coley and Barnes removed the cuffs and withdrew from the room while my senses were swimming. They're on the other side of the glass now, with the guys and gals of the Board. No guards in sight.

'This used to be the dining hall,' Dan-Dan tells me. He's pawing the glass, like a puppy waiting for a treat. 'The Wardroom was reserved for the officers. This was for the common crew. I prefer the informal atmosphere here. How about you?'

I try to tell him where he can stuff his *informal atmosphere*, but my mouth isn't working properly yet. All that comes out is a low mumbling noise.

'You haven't broken her, have you?' Dan-Dan snaps at Barnes and Coley. 'If you have, we'll kill her and send you straight out to find another one for us. I want a fully functional, talking zombie. I won't settle for second best.'

'She'll be fine in a minute or two,' Barnes assures him.

'She'd better be,' Dan-Dan growls. 'Poor thing. Did they hurt you, little girl? Don't worry, Dan-Dan will make the pain go away. I'd kiss you better if I could. Dan-Dan loves his clever zombie, yes he does.'

'Heaven save us from simpletons,' Lady Jemima sighs. 'Maybe we should throw Daniel in there with her.'

'Careful,' Lord Luca snarls. 'That's my brother you're talking about.'

'I was only joking,' Lady Jemima says quickly. 'I adore him really.'

As the would-be rulers of the world snipe at one another, the door to my side of the room opens and two guards step in and move to either side. They train their guns on me and tell me to take a few steps back. When I've retreated, a zombie is hustled in by another guard. There's a collar around the zombie's neck, attached to a stiff lead, giving the guard plenty of space.

Yet another guard enters, with a second captive zombie, followed by three more. Then one last guard comes in. This guy's holding a taser like Coley's. He gives each zombie a quick burst. As they fall to the floor and writhe, their handlers set them free and slip out of the room. The pair with guns are the last to leave and they slam shut the door after themselves. While the zombies on the floor recover, I study them cautiously. Three men, a woman and a teenage boy. The men are muscular and dressed in normal clothes. The woman is wearing a chef's outfit. The boy is naked.

'I chose that one,' Dan-Dan sniggers. 'Nudity is so pleasing to the eye, isn't it, especially in one so young and pure?'

'You're a degenerate,' Lord Luca laughs.

'Not at all,' Dan-Dan tuts. 'I simply like to appreciate the human form in all its natural glory.'

'An interesting mix,' Justin murmurs, then calls out to me. 'As the street-smart young woman that you appear to be, I'm sure you've already sussed the state of play. We want you to fight to the death. We've been pitting living slaves against zombies for months now, but they've struggled to stage an engaging fight. It seems the true gladiatorial spirit died out among the human masses long ago. But we're sure you'll serve up a decent show.'

I slide my jaw from side to side and wriggle my tongue about to make sure I can speak again. Then I shoot Justin the finger. 'Get stuffed, grandad.'

Justin shakes his head bitterly. 'Why do the youth of today have to make it so hard on themselves? Vicky, would you lend me your assistance?'

'My pleasure.' She moves to a small hatch which I hadn't noticed before. It's covered with a glass rectangle. She slides it open and draws a gun from a holster behind her back, kneels and aims at one of the male zombies.

'Fight or we'll kill him,' Justin says.

I shrug. 'You want me to kill him anyway, so what's the difference?'

'If you fight him, he stands a chance,' Justin says. 'And if he comes up short, at least he can die with honour.'

'I couldn't care less about honour,' I sniff.

'Do it,' Justin yaps and Vicky fires three times in quick succession. The man's head explodes and he slumps, truly dead now. The zombies around him snarl and dart at the hatch, angered by the attack and tempted by the scent of human brain. They slam into the glass but it barely quivers. Vicky shuts the hatch and moves to another—there are several of them set in the panels in different areas.

'Oh my God!' I scream, covering my ears with my hands. 'You did it! I didn't think you'd really do it!'

'We never bluff,' The Prince drawls, smiling as if he'd just won a war.

'Well, I don't either,' I jeer, lowering my hands and dropping the hysterical act. 'You lot are mugs. What do you think I am, zombie Spartacus or something? I don't give a toss about these walking corpses. Shoot them, fry them, chop them up into pieces if you want. I don't care.'

Justin frowns. 'You won't stand up to protect your own?'

'They're nothing to do with me,' I tell him. 'I don't have anything in common with these brain-dead abominations. Hell, I've finished off plenty of them myself over the last few months.'

'Interesting,' Justin murmurs. 'Then I suppose we'll have

242

to try a different tack. Daniel, will you go and fetch us one of your darlings?'

'Yes, yes, yes, yes, yes!' Dan-Dan crows. 'I was hoping for this. But I want to be the one who does it if she forces our hand. They're mine. I won't let Vicky or any of the others cheat me out of my prize.'

'Perish the thought,' Justin says. 'The honour will be all yours.'

'In that case, I'll be back before you can blink.' Dan-Dan shoots out of the room as if in a hurry to get to a party.

'Is this really necessary?' The Prince asks with a pained look.

'Yes,' Justin says.

'It would have been so much simpler if you'd just fought when asked,' The Prince admonishes me.

'What's happening?' Coley asks Justin. 'Where did Lord Wood go?'

'To bring us something truly dreadful,' Justin whispers, his eyes dark and sad, yet bright and excited at the same time.

FOURTEEN

Dan-Dan returns several minutes later and my heart sinks. Or would, if I had one.

He has a couple of kids with him, and both of them are alive.

'These are my darlings,' Dan-Dan coos, rubbing their heads and pointing them towards me. 'Say hello, my dears.'

The children mumble a frightened hello. One is a boy, the other a girl. Neither is more than seven or eight years old. They're dressed in sailor suits similar to Dan-Dan's. The boy looks like he's been crying. The girl's eyes are dry but she's clearly scared. Both are trembling.

'What's going on?' Barnes asks sharply.

'Surely you must have heard the rumours back in the day about the child-killer Daniel Wood?' Justin chuckles.

'Children had a habit of meeting with an unfortunate end

whenever Daniel came to town,' Vicky trills. 'He was such a naughty little boy.'

'My darlings,' Dan-Dan beams, hugging the children. 'They keep me company. I have nightmares when I'm by myself. My playmates help me keep body and soul together.'

'The trouble is, Daniel plays rough,' Lady Jemima notes, smiling cynically.

'He kills each child in the end, when he grows bored of them,' Justin grunts.

'Allegedly,' Lord Luca beams. 'Nothing was ever proven in a court of law. Why, he was never even prosecuted.'

Vicky Wedge winks at me. 'The advantage of having an unholy amount of money, and associates like me in high places.'

'You never told me any of this before,' Barnes snaps.

'Why should we?' Justin yawns. 'You're hired help.' He turns his attention to me. 'Now, Becky Smith, you might not care about the dead, but what about the living? Will you fight or does Daniel have to start squeezing?'

Dan-Dan slides his arms up and locks them round the children's throats. The girl begins to cry. Dan-Dan smiles darkly.

'It's always sad when I have to bid a darling goodbye,' he croaks. 'I miss each and every one. I used to keep a list of their names, but it grew so long . . .'

'You won't do it,' I say weakly.

'As I already told you, we never bluff,' The Prince murmurs but he sounds ashamed of his boast.

'Stop,' Barnes shouts. 'This is sick. I won't stand by and let you –'

'You will do what you're told!' Vicky Wedge screeches and aims her gun at him. Lord Luca, Lady Jemima and The Prince draw weapons too. Coley curses and darts behind Barnes.

'Don't shoot!' Coley cries. 'I'm on your side!'

Barnes stands firm, eyes filled with fury and contempt.

Justin gazes serenely at Barnes. 'There's no need for the guns,' he says to the others. 'Our man Barnes is smarter than that. He knows there are guards outside. They are armed and he is not. If he threatened us, they would execute him. The children too.'

'This is wrong,' Barnes snarls. 'You can't use innocent children this way.'

'Of course we can,' Justin snorts. 'We make the laws. We can do anything we want.'

'If it's any comfort to you, they're orphans,' Lady Jemima says. 'We have them delivered from camps. We only pick those who have no one to worry about them. We're not complete monsters.'

'You always did have a soft heart, my lovely,' Justin murmurs and turns his back on the glaring but impotent Barnes. 'We're waiting for your answer, Becky.'

'He's going to kill them in the end anyway,' I say softly.

'Probably,' Justin nods. 'But there's always a chance that he will take pity on these two. Or they might escape.'

'Oh, they never escape,' Dan-Dan whispers.

'There are others,' Lord Luca says.

'Fourteen or fifteen the last time I checked,' Vicky purrs.

'If you don't please us, he'll kill this pair and fetch replacements,' The Prince adds glumly.

'He can be very petulant when he doesn't get his way,' Lady Jemima concludes.

Both children are trying to tear free of Dan-Dan's grip. They're old enough to know what's going on. Dan-Dan is sweating with delight, his muscles bulging. I think he wants me to defy him, so that he can kill openly, like a disgusting, spoilt brat who wants to show off his latest vile habit.

'If I do this,' I say hollowly, 'I want to see the children every day, the whole group, so I can be sure that he hasn't killed any of them.'

'Hold on a minute,' Dan-Dan yaps. 'You're in no position to make demands.'

'Yes she is,' Justin overrides him. 'Agreed.'

'No!' Dan-Dan howls. 'They're mine. I'll do what I want with them.'

'Not under *my* watch,' Justin says, features darkening. 'This isn't a democracy. The girl is something new, something different. If you have to stop killing for a few weeks or months, to entice her to play ball, so be it. You're not going to spoil things for the rest of us.'

'Luca …' Dan-Dan whines, looking to his brother for support.

Lord Luca shrugs. 'I'm with Justin this time. I'm bored of the same old pathetic show, humans failing miserably every time we stick them in with the undead. I crave savage duels, heated action, true drama. If the girl has a reason to battle on – if she's fighting for others, not just herself – it will be all the more interesting.'

'You can have your darlings eventually,' Vicky says soothingly. 'We're not taking them away from you forever. You just need to be patient.'

'Oh, very well,' Dan-Dan pouts, releasing the children and pushing them aside. 'But I won't forget this. The next time one of you asks for a favour, don't expect me to jump.'

The Prince gathers the children from Dan-Dan and escorts them to the door, where he passes them to a guard who takes them back to their quarters.

'You can leave as well if you wish,' Justin says to Barnes. 'I won't make you watch if it offends you. This was meant to be a reward for services rendered, not a punishment.'

Barnes studies the businessman, stares at the open doorway, then looks back at me and shrugs. 'I was only worried about the kids. Now that we've dealt with that issue, I'm keen to stick around.'

'Excellent,' Justin beams. 'Becky, can you agitate them by yourself or do you need some help?'

'I've got it,' I mutter, flexing my fingers and preparing for battle.

I let my gaze linger on the undead men and woman for a moment, then stare glumly at the teenage boy. They're all standing with their backs to me, trying to gouge through the glass, unaware of the threat behind them. It would be easy to step up and drive my hands through their skulls, kill them all before they could react. But that wouldn't satisfy the bloodthirsty members of the Board. They want action and excitement, and it's my job to deliver that for them.

'Mum would be proud,' I snort. 'She always wanted me to go into showbiz.' Then, to cheers of encouragement from the inhuman humans, I sweep forward and attack.

FIFTEEN

I grab the collars of the men's shirts and haul them away from the glass. I kick the boy in the chest and send him sprawling. I slap the woman's face.

The zombies snarl and regroup. They stare at me, sniffing the air. They know I'm undead, so they're not sure why I've assaulted them. Zombies don't turn on one another. They find the peaceful unity in death that is so rare in life.

'Come on,' I growl, crooking my fingers at them. 'I'm not as dead as I look.'

They hiss and move closer, then stall and stare again. They can tell I'm not the same as them – no regular zombie can talk – but I'm more like them than the humans. They're reluctant to strike, seeing me as one of their own.

'Don't just stand there,' Dan-Dan calls, banging his fist on the glass. 'Make them angry.'

I give him the finger, then dart forward. I kick the boy in

the chest again and scratch the cheek of the nearest man. He instinctively throws a fist at me. I block it and punch him hard in the stomach.

The woman in the chef's outfit grabs my head and shakes it, pulling me away from the men. The boy leaps at me, growling like a dog. I kick him between the legs. Because he's naked, I have a clear shot. Every guy on the other side of the glass gasps and cringes. Then they cheer and clap.

I shrug off the woman and race towards a nearby pole. The men follow. I jump into the air, grab the pole and whirl around. I stick my legs out and my right foot connects with one of the men's jaw. His head snaps back and he staggers away.

'Oh, nice shot,' The Prince applauds. 'We never saw any of the others execute a move like that.'

'It's like watching a wrestling match,' Lady Jemima cackles.

'Only the result isn't fixed,' Justin laughs.

I tune out the babbling members of the Board and stay focused. Any one of these zombies could slice my skull open. I can't afford to get cocky.

The boy shambles towards me, still grimacing from the kick between his legs. I hate doing this to him, but the shot is there to be taken, so I swing my foot back, then kick him square in the nuts again.

'Unbelievable!' Lord Luca hoots.

'He'll be a eunuch by the end of this,' Vicky Wedge sniggers.

'It's bringing tears to my eyes,' Dan-Dan squeals, crossing his hands in front of his groin.

One of the men tackles me from behind and locks his arms across my chest. The other man charges me from the front. I lift my legs, clasp them around his neck in a scissor motion and snap it. He groans and wheels away, tugging at his head, trying to set it straight.

The man behind me squeezes, but there's no air in my lungs, so he doesn't do much damage. While he's trying to suffocate me, I twist my body the way I was trained by Master Zhang and throw him over my shoulder. He lands heavily in front of me. I make a blade of my fingers and drive my right hand through the centre of his forehead. He cries out, shudders, then falls still. I withdraw my hand and wipe it across his hair, cleaning my flesh of bits of the dead man's brain.

The woman slashes at me with the bones sticking out of her fingers. I block them with my own fingerbones, then jab at her eyes, forcing her back.

The boy lurches at me from the other side. He still hasn't properly protected his crown jewels, but I'm not able to find the angle to kick him a third time. He grabs me and digs his teeth into my left hip, tearing through my trousers, into the flesh.

I wince and club the boy over the head. His skull snaps and some of the flesh tears open. I spot brain and swiftly dig in, finishing him off. After the blows to his wedding tackle, I think death comes as a relative blessing.

The woman hurls herself at me, shrieking. For all I know, she was the boy's mother in life. Not that I think that factors into things now. She only wants to kill the beast who is threatening her. Zombies can't feel love, pity or affection. But they can feel fear. How unfair is that?

I shimmy out of the woman's way, slip in behind and get her in a stranglehold. She struggles furiously, but I was taught how to keep my grip tight. As she reels around the room with me on her back, I bare my fangs and bite into her skull. I chew loose a chunk of flesh and bone, and spit it out. I bite again. The woman mewls and shudders. After I tear away another chunk, there's enough space for me to jam in my chin, like a pig sticking its snout into a trough. I munch, rip and saw.

Seconds later the woman collapses beneath me and I push myself to my feet, spitting out brain. The brains of the undead do nothing for me. The taste is vile, nothing like the juicy, enticing brains of the living.

The only one left is the man with the broken neck. He doesn't provide much resistance. He's still trying to repair the damage to his spinal cord. I simply have to pad up behind him and crack his head open.

I step away from the last of the corpses and gaze at my handiwork. Four dead zombies, in addition to the one Vicky killed. It probably didn't take me more than a couple of minutes to fell them.

The members of the Board are cheering warmly. I glance at them numbly, blood on my hands, brains dribbling from my lips. The Prince winks at me. Lord Luca gives me the thumbs up. Justin claps louder than the others and shouts over the noise, 'Ladies and gentlemen, a gladiator is born!'

The nightmare begins for real.

SIXTEEN

It's been a week or more since I wound up in the clutches of the Board. A week of almost non-stop fighting, with rests only to allow my captors to sleep, eat and indulge in their other pastimes.

When I'm not needed, I'm kept in a room near the fore of the cruiser, in what used to be known as a mess. A few hammocks are slung across it. I lie in one of those when I'm relaxing, sometimes for hours without moving, staring at the ceiling with my unblinking eyes, trying to think of a way out of this horror show.

In an ideal world I'd kill the creeps of the Board, free the children and slip away into the night. Since I'm unlikely to score on all three fronts, I'd settle for murdering the manip-ulative monsters who think they're superior to the rest of us.

But there's not much chance of that. They keep them-selves separate. I usually only see them in the converted dining hall when they want me to kill. And then they're always safe behind their wall of glass. Many of my opponents have tried to smash through that wall. I've even thrown a few of them at it with all my strength while fighting, to test it. Not so much as a crack. It's tough as steel.

The battles have drained me. Zombies are more resilient than humans, but we're not inexhaustible. We wear down. I've fought four or five times most days, usually against a handful of opponents, but sometimes as many as eight. I'm not stronger than those I've come up against, but I'm sharper. I can outwit and outmanoeuvre them.

Even so, I've suffered my share of injuries. I've broken several bones. My neck and chest have been slashed, chunks bitten out of my arms and legs. A couple of teeth were smashed from my gums—that *really* hurt and still does.

Justin spoke of keeping me on for months when I first arrived, but I'll be lucky to last a fortnight, maybe a bit longer if they reduce the number of daily bouts. I'm a short-term project for them.

I wasn't going to tell them that I need brains to function, that I'll regress if I don't eat. But they know that zombies need to feed to stay sharp, so they supplied me with brains without my having to ask for them, a couple of days after I'd fallen into their foul clutches. Coley delivered the first batch.

'Barnes and I rustled these up from corpses on the streets,' he told me. 'Not my idea of a good time, but anything to please our lords and ladies.'

'What if I don't want to eat?' I said in a low voice.

Coley shrugged. 'They'll see that as a sign of mutiny and give me the order to put you out of your misery. Which is fine by me, so go ahead and refuse.'

I made a sighing noise and dug in. I wouldn't have been able to resist for long anyway, not once the brains had been set before me. I'd seen it in the zom heads when they were starved. As you approach the end of consciousness, you lose control. In a few days I'd have dug into the brains regardless.

'Dan-Dan didn't want us to go foraging for used brains,' Coley said as I threw up the remains of the brains once I'd absorbed the nutrients from them. 'He had a more novel idea. He wanted to put one of the guards in with you, make you kill him and eat his fresh brain. He's some piece of work, isn't he? Makes Barnes and me look like a pair of saints. You didn't know how lucky you were when we were the worst you had to deal with.'

Coley got that much right. Dan-Dan is a real beauty, full of unpleasant ideas. He came to see me the day after my first fight. Six guards flanked him and he kept well back. He wanted me to wear a revealing leather outfit, the sort you used to find in seedy adult shops.

'Not a hope in hell,' I told him.

'I'll kill one of my darlings if you don't wear it,' he huffed.

'That threat won't work this time,' I dismissed him. 'I'll tell Justin and refuse to fight in protest. The others wouldn't like that, would they?'

'You're no fun,' Dan-Dan pouted, then slunk away like the disgusting rat that he is.

Even given my functioning brain, I'd have come unstuck long before now if not for my training. Master Zhang taught me well. I zing around that room like a pinball, striking swiftly, slipping out of reach before my foes can counter. I'm improving all the time, learning new tricks, finding a whole string of ways to attack and defend. I'd be proud of how I've performed if I wasn't so sickened by what is being asked of me.

The living dead deserve better than this. I don't have a lot of sympathy for zombies. They're killers by nature. But they didn't ask for reanimation or the hunger that drives them. They're not responsible for their actions. The rest of us, on the other hand, are. And what we're doing here is disgraceful. Sure, I've killed reviveds before, like in the tunnel under Waterloo Station, but that was to prepare for a battle with evil. It wasn't for sport.

I tried wriggling off the hook a couple of days ago. I carefully dropped my guard while fighting, moved a bit slower than I could, let myself be pummelled. That's when I lost the teeth. I'd planned to lose a whole lot more, to let my opponents carve me up. But Vicky got wise to what I was plotting.

'You can do better than that, Miss Smith,' she called out as I circled three undead guys, each double the size of me.

'Why don't you come in and try if you think it's that easy?' I snarled.

'That will not be necessary,' she retaliated. 'I can see what you're up to. The stench of treachery is thick in the air. You want out. Rest assured, if you are defeated today, every one of Dan-Dan's darlings will be executed within the hour. And it will not be swift or painless.'

I cursed Vicky Wedge and the rest of them, but they had me by the short and curlies. There was nothing for it but to up my game and fight for real. I came out the undefeated champion, but the victory cost me dear. I've been hobbling in pain ever since.

The door to my room opens and I raise myself, groaning, ready to fight again. But no guards enter this time. Instead it's Barnes. I haven't seen him since that day when I was first presented to the Board.

'Come to gloat?' I snarl, letting myself fall back into my hammock.

'No,' he says, taking a seat. I'm not chained up, so I could attack him, but he doesn't look afraid. Either he's sure I'll leave him be out of fear of reprisal, or he's confident that he could draw his gun and open fire before I got my hands on him.

'Come to take my order then? Cool. I'll have my brains fried, sunny side up.'

Barnes grins. 'I'll pass your request on to Coley.'

'Where is your trusty sidekick?' I ask.

'Taking it easy. Having some fun.'

'I thought he might be cowering behind you again.'

Barnes chuckles. 'That wasn't his finest moment. I haven't brought it up with him yet, but I certainly plan to. I'm just waiting for the right time.'

'This is all screwed,' I mutter. 'I don't care what these guys are doing for you, nothing can justify this. You've sided with a pack of demons. Dan-Dan torments and kills children. How can you live with yourself, serving a beast like that?'

'I don't have to explain my motives to the likes of you,' Barnes grunts. 'You killed plenty of kids yourself, I'm sure, when you turned.'

'That's different. I couldn't control myself. I can now. You can too. But you choose not to.'

'Our choices are sometimes limited,' Barnes sighs, then shakes his head and squints at me. 'Enough of the soul-baring. I'm here to offer you a deal.'

'This should be interesting,' I sneer.

'You've lost your sheen,' Barnes says. 'You're slowing up.

The constant fighting has taken it out of you. You're slow to heal – if you heal at all – and your wounds are weakening you. Our lords and ladies have started to worry. They enjoy watching you in action. They don't want to lose their prize plaything.'

'Tell them if they love me, they should set me free,' I say sweetly.

Barnes laughs. 'I like you, Becky, I truly do. You've got more balls than most of the guys I've ever known. I want to help you if I can.'

I cock an eyebrow at the hunter. 'If you're looking to break me out, I'm all ears.'

Barnes smiles wryly. 'I don't like you *that* much. But I've come up with a compromise that might work. The Board want me to find other zombies like you, who can speak and think. They want to see you take on one of your own, some-one who can mount a genuine challenge. They've instructed me to find a few of your friends, like the ones I saw you with in Leicester Square.'

I flash my teeth at him. 'I don't have any *friends*.'

'Then you won't mind if I find some of the gang you were with, bring them back here and force you to fight them,' he says calmly.

I glare at him and don't respond.

'*Or*,' Barnes says teasingly, 'we can strike a deal.'

'What's this deal you keep going on about?' I sniff.

'Simple,' he says. 'Tell me where your colleagues are. I'll round up the lot of them. Then we'll set you free.'

I smother a laugh. 'You expect me to believe you'd let me go?'

'I'm not a liar.'

'But you're also not the main man here. Not even close. The lords and ladies of the Board would never sanction my release.'

'They already have,' Barnes says. 'I took the offer to them before I came to you. Said I didn't think you'd go for it, but that I wanted to know where they stood if you did. They voted four to two in your favour. I won't tell you who voted against you, as I'd hate to sour the special relationship you have with them.'

'What makes you think they'd honour their pledge?' I ask.

'Easier to do that than betray me. They might not think much of me as a man, but they respect me as a soldier. Besides, I'm useful to them. There will be other ways I can help them further down the line. You have my guarantee that we'll make good on our promise.'

I don't really have to think about it, but I give myself a minute to mull it over, just to be absolutely sure of my answer. When I've decided, I smirk and rock in my hammock. 'Sorry, Barnes. Couldn't help you even if I wanted. Like I told the Board, we moved around all the time. We don't have a base. I've no idea where they might be.'

Barnes nods and stands. 'I expected nothing more but felt I owed you the offer. I'll find them anyway. Hunting's what I excel at. I'll track them down, subdue them and drag their sorry asses back here.

'I hope those conscious zombies truly aren't your friends. Because soon you're going to have to face them in the arena and kill or be killed. And there's nothing worse than having to sacrifice someone you care about. Take it from one who knows.'

On that enigmatic note he leaves and, as I carry on rocking, I reflect bitterly on the fact that my future, as short as it was already given my dire situation, probably just got a hell of a lot shorter.

SEVENTEEN

I'm marched down to see the children every day. They're being held on the deck beneath mine. They sleep in bunk beds. The boiler room is nearby and that's where they play and exercise. I usually view them there. They're pale from lack of sunlight and haggard-looking, but they seem to be enjoying their respite and have been a bit cheerier every day.

There are fifteen of them, mostly boys, but some girls too. I never get to spend a lot of time with them and we don't talk much. But at least I can see that they're alive and being taken care of. For however long I might last.

It's been nine or ten days since Barnes made his offer. Part of me wishes I'd accepted. I was telling the truth when I said I didn't have any friends among the Angels. That was the advantage of keeping my distance. I could have sold them out, walked away a free girl, put this episode behind me and tried to forget about the Board and my treachery.

But, as bad as things get, I never really regret telling Barnes to get stuffed. I don't want to see out the rest of my days as a Judas, especially given the fact that I might live for a few thousand years. There are some things you can never forget or forgive yourself for.

Mind you, I won't have to worry about thousands of years in my current state. I've taken several severe hammerings over the last week. I'm getting sluggish. I can't move as swiftly as I did, or react as sharply as I could at my peak. I'm running on willpower alone these days. If it wasn't for the children, I'd give up the ghost. But I've got to buy them as much time as I can. A few days won't make any difference to me, but it might to them.

I watch the children running round the boiler room, smiling softly to myself as they play hide-and-seek. I wish the guards would leave me here for an hour or two, but they never allow me more than a few minutes, just enough time to do a headcount and satisfy myself that they're all as well as they can be given the wretched circumstances.

'Aren't they wonderful?' someone murmurs behind me.

I glance over my shoulder and my smile disappears. It's Dan-Dan. He's wearing a fireman's outfit today. It doesn't fit him any better than his sailor's costume.

'Why don't you get clothes the right size?' I growl. 'Nobody wants to look at your belly.'

'*I* like looking at it,' he giggles. 'And I like my tight clothes. They feel much better when they're cutting into me.'

He moves forward, careful not to get too close. My arms are tied behind my back and my ankles are shackled together, but I still pose a threat and Dan-Dan is all too aware of it. Keeping a safe distance, he stops at a railing and studies the children.

'I miss them so much,' he sighs. 'You have no idea how lonely and scared I get when I'm by myself. I never have nightmares when I torture and kill. And the nightmares are so terrifying ...'

'Stop,' I whimper. 'You'll make me cry.'

'I don't expect you to understand,' he says. 'Hardly anyone does. All I can tell you is that I bitterly regret the day I let you convince me to stop killing in order to watch you fight. The fighting bores me now.'

'It doesn't bore the others,' I note.

'Not yet,' he concedes. 'But their interest will wane soon, as mine has. They'll discard you like a dull blade once Barnes returns with fresh, intelligent zombies. Even if he can't find any, I don't think you'll enjoy their favour much longer. They're tired of your face. Nobody likes watching the same person triumph all the time. We only endure your victories because they'll make your ultimate defeat so much sweeter when it comes.'

'Maybe I won't lose. Maybe I'll win every time, go on for years. What do you think of that, Fireman Dan?'

Dan-Dan shakes his head and smirks. 'We can all see that you're close to the end. It's been fascinating, watching your energy ebb away. Educational too. We never knew a zombie could be worn down like one of the living. We've learnt a lot by studying you. I think we'll push your replacements less strenuously, make them last longer.'

Dan-Dan turns and stands with his back to the railing. 'By the way, they won't let you die in the arena. When you reach the stage where you can't fight any longer, they're going to hand you over to me.'

'What are you talking about?' I snap.

'I told them I couldn't bear it,' he giggles. 'Said I was going mad, not being able to kill. I demanded access to my darlings. To keep me quiet, they've offered you to me instead of the children. When you run out of steam, the guards will drag you out of there before you're killed. They'll tie you up neatly and deliver you to my personal quarters. I have so many things I want to share with you before the end.'

'You won't get your filthy hands on me,' I snarl. 'I'll let the zombies kill me first.'

'You think so?' Dan-Dan grins. 'It won't be easy. If they could slit your throat open and finish you off that way, you might stand a chance. But they have to dig through your skull and tear out your brain, chunk by chunky chunk. That takes time. We'll shoot them before they rip you apart. Vicky and Luca will save you. For me.'

Dan-Dan's grin fades and he takes a step closer. 'You probably think you know pain intimately. But let me tell you, little girl, you don't. I'm going to put you through a whole new universe of torment before I grant you blessed release. I'm in no rush, and you can take so much more than any of my darlings. I might keep you writhing around on a leash for weeks. Imagine that, weeks of delirious suffering, where every moment is agony redefined and writ large.'

'Screw you,' I moan.

Dan-Dan smiles again. 'No,' he says breezily. 'You're the one who's screwed. I'm looking forward to working with you more closely, Becky. You will be my masterpiece. The one to whom I reveal the true, unfathomable depths of my twisted fury. When I set to work on you, the results might shock even me.

'Toodle-pip!'

With a sick chuckle, he slides past and exits, leaving me in the boiler room with his darlings. Their excited cries as they search for each other don't sound quite so cheery now. In fact they sound eerily like the screams of the damned.

EIGHTEEN

I'm led into the arena for another gruelling bout. I keep hoping that the guards will grow careless. I've gone along with them meekly each time, acting as if my spirits have been crushed, obeying their every command, eager to please. Praying that they might stop regarding me as a threat. All I need is a small slip, a glimmer of a chance.

But so far they've followed their guidelines impeccably. They truss me up expertly, slip a collar round my neck and check the steel lead a few times before forcing me out of the mess. There are always extra guards around, guns cocked and aimed, ready to cut me down if I revolt.

'Here's our girl,' Dan-Dan chortles as I'm guided in. He's back in his sailor's costume. The other zombies are already in place, still held captive by their guards. They always release us at the same time, so they can exit together.

'How have you been, my dear?' Lady Jemima asks, faking

concern. 'You were struck a nasty blow last time. We were worried about you.'

'I'm fine,' I mutter, trying to ignore the throbbing at the back of my head where I was clubbed in my previous fight.

'You don't look too lively,' Justin says critically. 'Perhaps you'd like to sit this one out? We can send you back to the mess if you'd prefer.'

I'd love a good rest but I'm wary. I don't think I'll be returned to the mess if they judge me too weary to fight. Once they reckon I've run out of steam, I figure I'll be delivered straight to Dan-Dan's quarters.

'Nothing wrong with me,' I sniff. 'I'm all fired up and raring to go.'

'Very well,' Justin smiles. 'Release the beasts.'

Our handlers taser us, set us free and retreat. Once I've recovered from the shock, I roll my arms around, limbering up, and check out my latest batch of opponents as they surge towards the glass and paw at the panels, trying to break through to the six smug humans on the other side.

There are seven zombies, five men and two women. Each looks like they had plenty of experience of fighting when they were alive. One of the women is wearing a karate outfit. She must have been training or taking part in a competition when she was attacked.

I've faced all sorts of opponents here, but most have been

bruisers like this lot, especially in recent battles. The Board are pushing me to my limits, waiting for me to break.

'I bet she comes undone this time,' Lady Jemima says as she studies the muscles on the two zombies closest to her.

'How much?' The Prince asks.

'This,' she says, flashing a diamond ring at him.

'Nice.' The Prince whistles. 'If you throw in the rest of the rings on that hand, I'll wager my crown.'

'Done,' Lady Jemima smirks.

'I didn't think you would risk so treasured a possession,' Vicky Wedge notes.

The Prince shrugs. 'There will be plenty of crowns to choose from when the world is ours.'

I decide to get things under way. I move forward wearily and make a nuisance of myself, angering the zombies, luring them away from the glass, focusing their attention on me.

We begin our waltz of death. Once they're riled up, I manipulate every last section of the arena, buzzing around like a fly, grabbing poles and whipping myself into the air, utilising the walls and ceiling as much as the floor. I know this area inside out and I use that knowledge to my advantage.

I jump and grab hold of one of the overhead pipes as two of the men charge towards me. From that position I can lash out at both of them at the same time with my feet.

A couple of poles are set close together in one zone. I

grab the woman in the karate outfit and propel her towards them, then angle her head down and ram it between the poles, jamming her in place. I leave her there, stuck, to finish off at the end when I'm done with the others.

I barge one of the men into a wall at a point which I've identified as a possible weak spot. The steel panel always shakes when someone is thrown against it. I keep hoping that it will tear loose completely one day, but no joy so far. Today it rattles as usual but holds.

The members of the Board keep up a running commentary. They're sipping champagne, casually discussing the battle, their plans for the future, what they fancy for dinner. They're a boring, self-obsessed lot. I'd rather total silence, but I can't tell them that or they'd talk all the louder just to spite me.

The other female zombie snags the hole in my chest with her fingerbones and tears five nasty channels through the flesh down towards my belly button.

'Yowzers!' Dan-Dan howls happily as I roar with pain.

'That's got to hurt,' Lord Luca chuckles.

I kick the woman away and flee to the far side of the arena, gritting my teeth. I quickly examine the wounds to make sure no guts are spilling out. Then I leap over the head of one of the onrushing men. But I don't get as much height as I thought I would. He clips my legs and drags me to the ground, then bellows and smashes a fist at my face. The bones jutting out of his fingers glint in the light. If he connects, it's game over and at least I won't have to worry about ending up in the clutches of Dan-Dan.

But it's impossible to lie still and let myself be killed. My defences kick in automatically. I knock the man's hand aside and twist my head in the opposite direction. His fist slams into the floor and instead of breaking my skull, he breaks a few of the bones in his fingers.

I scramble to my feet and stagger away from the other reviveds, who are all closing in on me, except for the trapped woman. A long strip of ducting runs the length of what was once the dining hall. I jump and haul myself up, wedging myself between the ducting and the ceiling. There's just enough space for me. I've squeezed in here before when I've needed a rest.

The zombies punch the base and sides of the ducting, trying to grab hold and pull me down. But they can't get at me, except to scratch the sides of my arms and legs. If a few of them climbed up, the ducting would come crashing to the floor, leaving me at the mercy of my foes. But thankfully they aren't smart enough to work that out.

'No fair,' Dan-Dan shouts, slapping the glass. 'I hate it when she does that. Why can't we take that ducting out of there?'

'Now now,' Justin tuts. 'We have to give her a reasonable

chance. It's more fun this way. She can't stay up there forever.'

I've tried crawling through the ducting at either end, but both exits have been sealed. Still, when I'm up here, I usually creep to one end or the other to hurl a few blows at the bolted-on steel plates, just in case there's any give.

I start pulling myself along like an injured snake. The zombies follow beneath me, scraping at the ducting, gurgling furiously. I wonder if they hate me more than the humans, if they see me as a traitor to the undead cause.

As I'm mulling that over and trying to tune out Dan-Dan's jeers, the sound of gunfire echoes down from the deck above. Nobody takes any notice of it at first. The guards on the upper deck often fire at passing zombies, or even at corpses floating down the river, for practice. But this time it doesn't stop after a few seconds as it normally does. It's sustained. Then, moments later, mingled in with the gunfire, I hear what might just be the sweetest noise ever.

Human screams.

The lords and ladies of the Board have fallen silent. They're staring at the open doorway on their side of the glass divide, heads cocked, jaws slack. They don't look like the masters and mistresses of the universe any more.

The zombies keep slapping at the ducting, unaware of the change of play. I ignore them and stare at the doorway along with the living.

A guard spills into the narrow corridor, falls over, then clambers to his feet. His face is contorted with terror. 'We're under attack!' he shouts.

'Who the hell dares attack us?' Justin barks, recovering his power of speech. 'Is it the army?'

The guard shakes his head. 'Zombies, I think. But we're not sure. They came from the river. They've swarmed the deck. I don't think we can hold for long.'

Justin curses foully, then draws a gun and shoots the startled guard through the middle of his forehead.

'Why did you do that?' The Prince shrieks.

'I don't spare messengers when they bring bad news,' Justin growls, then hops over the dead guard and into the corridor beyond.

The Prince stares at the corpse. There's another extended blast of gunfire overhead. He flinches, then hurries after Justin. Vicky, Lord Luca and Dan-Dan scramble after the first pair of deserters. Lady Jemima just sinks to the floor and covers her head with her hands. She starts moaning, 'No, no, no. This wasn't part of the plan. It can't happen like this. I won't let it. This is *our* world.'

Dan-Dan pauses in the doorway as the others flee. He looks back at me. I'm stunned to see him smirking. 'Isn't this exciting?' he coos.

'Run, run as fast you can, fat boy,' I snarl. 'But it won't make any difference. You're history.'

Dan-Dan snorts. 'I think not, little girl. I have more lives than a cat. See you later, alligator.'

'It'll be sooner than you'd like, crocodile.'

Dan-Dan winks. 'I'll be looking forward to the day.'

He skips out, laughing, leaving me to fend off the zombies and wait for whoever or whatever is coming.

NINETEEN

My gut instinct is that Mr Dowling and his mutants are orchestrating the attack. They set me free from prison once before when all seemed lost, and came to my rescue in Leicester Square when it looked like my goose was cooked. They're making a habit of saving my sorry neck from the chop. Long may it continue! I just hope they don't decide to kill me this time. Mr Dowling has shown mercy previously for some unknowable reason, but there's no telling which way the demented clown will blow when the wind changes direction.

I hang tight to the ducting and wait for the mutants or their master to find me. I'm hoping creepy Owl Man isn't with them. Then the door opens and a familiar figure bursts into the room and I realise my gut was just about as wrong as wrong can be.

'*Rage!*' I yell, for once with delight instead of contempt.

Rage squints at me. 'What are you doing up there?'

'This is what I do for kicks,' I growl. 'Now quit gawping and help me, will you?'

'Wait a minute,' Rage says and steps outside. 'She's here,' he hollers, then returns and lays into the zombies.

As Rage shoves the zombies away from me and starts cracking their heads open, Dr Oystein comes running into the room. 'B!' he cries, hurrying to where I'm hanging. He offers me his hand and helps me down.

'Nice to see you, doc,' I mutter.

'You too,' he says politely, then embraces me with a surprisingly strong bear hug. 'I thought we had lost you forever.'

'You don't get rid of me that easily,' I chuckle, and hug him in return, burying my face in his chest, wishing I could cry so that I could blink back tears.

The twins race into the room as Dr Oystein releases me. They're dripping wet but they look ecstatic.

'We've taken control of the deck,' Cian cheers.

'Some of the guards are still fighting, but we have them trapped,' Awnya says.

'Master Zhang has started a sweep of the lower decks,' Cian adds. 'He says you should be cautious until he is certain the ship is ours.'

'There are children on the deck below this,' I tell the twins. 'Make sure nobody hurts them. They were being held captive.'

'We know all about the children,' Dr Oystein calms me. 'We will take good care of them and escort them back to County Hall when we have concluded our business here.'

'How did you find me?' I ask. 'How did you board the ship? Where –'

A scream stops me short. I look up. An Angel has entered the viewing area on the other side of the glass. It's Ingrid, the Angel I went on my very first ever mission with. Lady Jemima is backing away from her, eyes wide, shaking her head wildly.

'Who's this?' Ingrid asks me.

'A bitch who needs putting down,' I growl.

'Glad to be of service,' Ingrid grunts and closes in on the whimpering Lady Jemima. The human shuts her eyes and starts to pray, but why would God heed the prayers of a she-devil? Moments later it's all over as far as Lady J is concerned.

I push myself away from Dr Oystein. 'There were five others. They dressed differently to the guards. Have you seen them?'

'I saw one on the deck,' Dr Oystein replies. 'He was dressed like a prince. He tried to make the gangway. He did not get very far.'

'I spotted a few heading down the stairs,' Rage says, pausing to address me over the heads of the zombies. 'One was dressed like a sailor.'

'*Dan-Dan*,' I growl and start for the door.

'B,' Dr Oystein calls me back. 'There are plenty of us onboard. We can handle this. You look drained and battered. You should rest.'

'I'll rest when those bastards are dead.' I grimace and flash the doc an apologetic smile. 'Sorry. I didn't mean to snap. But I need to do this. I want to make them pay for what they did to me.'

'I understand,' the doctor says, returning my smile. 'Good luck, B.'

'If you wait a minute, I can come with you,' Rage says, knocking another of the zombies to the floor.

'You're fine,' I tell him. 'This is something I'd rather do by myself.'

'Always the loner,' Rage laughs, bashing the heads of two more zombies together.

I want to respond to that but there isn't time. I'm worried that Dan-Dan and the rest of them might slip the net. Waving briefly to the doc and Rage, I slide out of the arena, a free girl for the first time since I came to this stinking cruiser, and head off in search of my captors. The tables have turned and I plan to put them through a whole heap of hurt before I break their rotten necks and rid this world of their unholy, stinking presence.

TWENTY

I hurry to the nearest set of stairs and practically throw myself down to the deck beneath. I pause and sniff the air. I can smell the children but no one from the Board. Of course my nose isn't infallible. If they raced fore or aft, I wouldn't be able to sniff them out from here. But I'm guessing they delved further into the bowels of the ship.

I carry on down to the next level. Gunfire starts afresh as I'm looking around. Screams. Master Zhang and his Angels must have found more guards. If the members of the Board are with them, they're finished. I just have to hope that they pressed on. If not, I'll find their corpses later and vomit over them to demonstrate my disgust.

Down another flight of stairs. The engine room is on this floor. I can't smell anything, but as I'm standing at the base of the stairs, weighing up my options, I hear a clanging noise. I move ahead cautiously, not getting my hopes up.

There are all sorts of people on the old cruiser, crew members, guards, zombies, Angels. There's no guarantee that one of the louses of the Board made the noise.

More gunfire overhead helps mask the sound of my footsteps. I come to the engine room and let myself in. The place is filled with banks of dials and switches. I've no idea what any of them do and I don't care. All that matters to me is the smell in the air, familiar and sweet the closer I draw.

I hear them before I see them. Lord Luca is muttering angrily. 'I told you we should have stuck with Justin and Vicky. It was madness branching off on our own.'

'They're the mad ones,' Dan-Dan replies merrily, as if he hadn't a care in the world. 'It was crazy, pushing on. We don't know how fast the zombies can move. I wouldn't want to get into a race with them. Better to get out of here as swiftly as we can.'

'But how?' Lord Luca shouts. 'I don't know which button we're supposed to press. I wasn't paying attention when they showed us. There were so many escape routes and options, I can't remember them all.'

'You never did have the keenest attention span,' Dan-Dan laughs.

'I don't see you doing any better, genius,' Lord Luca snaps.

I round a bank of dials and come in view of the pair. Lord Luca is standing before a wall of switches, desperately flicking every one that he can. Dan-Dan is standing behind him, giggling.

'Having fun, boys?' I murmur.

Their heads snap round. Lord Luca yelps and throws switches faster than before. Dan-Dan tips his hat at me and says, 'I didn't expect you to catch up with me this quickly.'

'I don't believe in wasting time,' I grin, taking a step towards them, savouring the moment, wanting to make it last.

'We can pay you!' Lord Luca shrieks. 'We'll give you any-thing you want!'

'There's only one thing she wants,' Dan-Dan chuckles, then grabs his brother by the arm and spins him towards me.

'No!' Lord Luca cries as he crashes to the floor in front of me. 'What are you doing? Help me, fool!'

'You're the fool,' Dan-Dan gurgles, rubbing his hairy belly, picking a crumb from it and placing it delicately on his outstretched tongue. 'I never did like you, Luca. You were weak and scatterbrained like Mother. Father always said he only kept you around in case he ever needed an organ trans-plant. Poor Papa was always worried about his kidneys and heart.'

Lord Luca gawps with disbelief at his grotesque brother, then gulps and stares up at me. His look of fear fades, to be replaced by one of calm resignation. 'Is there any point begging for mercy?' he asks.

'No,' I tell him, then grab the sides of his head and lower my mouth. I lick his forehead and rub my nose across it. He whimpers, fear creeping back across his expression again. Then I bite into his skull and gnaw through the bone into the brain beneath. I'd like to make it last longer, but I'm anxious to move on to Dan-Dan.

When Lord Luca stops moaning and struggling, I let his body drop and face Dan-Dan, wiping bits of his brother's brain from my lips. To my surprise, the child-killer is crying.

'It's silly, isn't it?' Dan-Dan weeps. 'I cried when Mother died too, even though I threw her to the zombies, just as I've thrown Luca to you. I'm too soft for this cruel world.'

'You won't have to worry about it for much longer,' I chuckle grimly.

He squints at me. 'You really are a beautifully fearsome creature. I'm sorry I didn't get a chance to go to work on you. There's so much more to you than any of my darlings. The sweet torments I could have put you through . . .'

'Sorry to disappoint you,' I hiss.

'No need to apologise,' he smiles. 'You were simply doing what you had to. I don't hold it against you. I'm not one to bear a grudge.'

'Well, the bad news is, I am.' I flex my fingers and advance. 'I'm gonna hurt you, Dan-Dan. It won't be quick like it was for Luca. You promised me a universe of pain. Well, you're gonna reap what you planned to sow. For what

284

you did to me and the children, I'm going to make it long and slow and painful.'

Dan-Dan shakes his head. 'I don't think so. You might want to torture me but you haven't the stomach for it. Few people have. I'm gifted. Emotions never got between me and my desires. I've always had the power to do whatever I wished.

'I'm going to miss you, Becky,' he says. 'What I wouldn't give to pinch your clammy cheek and kiss you goodnight as I put you to sleep forever. That time will come, I'm sure, but the days will be long and lonely without you until then.'

'Don't worry,' I tell him. 'You'll have plenty of company in Hell while you're waiting for me.'

'Oh, I'm not going to Hell just yet,' Dan-Dan says brightly. 'My brother was feather-headed. I was toying with him before you arrived. I wanted him to sweat. I always loved to wind up Luca. But I have a very good memory and I pay attention to the smallest of details. So, without further ado ...'

Dan-Dan reaches up and presses a switch. The wall behind him explodes. I cry out – with my sensitive hearing it's as if someone has struck a large bell with a hammer by the side of my head – and turn away instinctively. When the worst of the pain passes and I look again, Dan-Dan has leapt through a gaping hole in the side of the cruiser.

'Son of a bitch!' I roar, darting after him. I get to the hole, almost jump, but pull up short, not willing to throw myself into the great unknown. Instead, once I have control of myself again, I study the river beneath me.

Dan-Dan has landed in the water and is swimming towards a speedboat moored nearby. I think about jumping after him, but he has too great a lead on me. Reaching the boat, he climbs into it, starts the engine, waves nonchalantly at me, then powers away along the Thames, heading west.

'James bloody Bond,' I snarl. Then I laugh with grudging admiration. I hate that child-killing monster, but I have to admit he knows how to make a cool getaway.

As I watch Dan-Dan disappear into the sunset (well, it's not long after midday, but he's earned a bit of poetic licence), another chunk of the hull blows outwards and Justin Bazini and Vicky Wedge throw themselves into the river and make for a speedboat of their own. Now that I look closely, I realise there are several more tied to the ship. The lords and ladies of the Board had obviously planned for an invasion like this. I bet they never told the guards about the secret escape hatches. They wouldn't have considered their underlings worth saving.

Turning my back on the hole, I send a silent promise after Dan-Dan and the others. *We'll meet again, my wretched* darlings, *and you won't get away from me so easily next time.*

Then, still wincing from the noise of the explosion, I retrace my steps and head back up the stairs to see what's going on and discover how the Angels found me.

TWENTY-ONE

I pass Master Zhang as I'm climbing the stairs. He's moving in the opposite direction, down into the hold. He pauses to study me and I bow to him politely.

'You have been in the wars,' he notes.

'They made me fight several times every day,' I tell him.

He grunts. 'The fact that you survived this long proves that you were concentrating during your lessons.' Then he pushes on. I allow myself a wry chuckle. Master Zhang isn't a man to go wild with compliments.

I make my weary way to the arena. It's all quiet on the upper deck now. I want to run up there, get out of this prison as soon as I can. But Dr Oystein is waiting for me in the old dining hall. Answers first, release later.

When I get to the arena, I see that the doctor isn't the only one waiting for me. All of the Angels from my room are present, Ashtat, Carl, Shane, Jakob. Rage and the twins have hung around. Plus there's one more addition, but this guy isn't so welcome.

'*Barnes!*' I bellow, charging towards him, fingers tightening, meaning to do all the things to him that I can't do to the departed Dan-Dan.

Carl and Shane slide together to block my path.

'Easy,' Carl says.

'He's on our side,' Shane says.

'Never,' I bark. 'He only looks out for himself.'

I try to push through. Carl and Shane shove me back. I get ready to fight.

'It's true, B,' Dr Oystein says softly. 'He came to us at County Hall, told us what was happening here, led us to you.'

I stop struggling. If I could, I'd blink like an owl. Carl and Shane move apart. Barnes is standing directly ahead of me. He's taken the bullet from behind his ear and is tapping his front teeth with it. He raises an eyebrow when he spots my fingers clenching and unclenching.

'It's a real pisser when you don't know whether to thank a guy or spit in his eye, isn't it?' he smirks.

'I can't really spit these days,' I growl, 'but I'll never thank you either. What for—capturing me, enslaving me, bringing me here for Dan-Dan and the others to toy with?'

Barnes shrugs. 'As I told you before, our choices are sometimes limited. I have a son, Stuart, who means everything to me. He survived the attacks and was staying in a compound in the countryside. He was relatively safe there, but the compounds are no guarantee of long-term security. Several have fallen and others will too. When you're land-locked, you're always open to attack.

'I carried on hunting after my first run-in with you,' he continues. 'I made sure the zombies I killed weren't con-scious, but otherwise it was business as normal. The members of the Board heard about me. They invited me to come visit. I was curious, so I paid them a call. They wanted to employ me to find new gladiators for them. But they weren't interested in ordinary zombies. They'd heard rumours that I'd met one who could talk.'

'How did they hear about that?' I sneer.

'I never discussed it with anyone,' Barnes said, 'but Coley and the others who were with us that day did. The stories intrigued the Board. They offered me a king's ransom to deliver you to them.'

'And you jumped at the chance.'

Barnes sniffs. 'I never cared about money. I couldn't be bought that way. But every man has his price. Mine was the safety of my son.' He sighs and sticks the bullet back behind his ear. 'They offered Stuart a place on one of the islands which are free of zombies. I tried getting him on to one of those before, but it's virtually impossible to gain access. Justin and his cronies operate several islands. If I agreed to work for them, they promised to ship out Stuart. I didn't even have to think about it.'

I glare at the hunter, still wanting to hate him, but finding myself thawing. If he's telling the truth, I understand. In his position I'd have done the same.

'So why the change of heart?' I scowl. 'Why play the hero now after serving the scumbags for so long?'

'The children,' Barnes says softly. 'I didn't know about them until they let me in here to watch you fight. A zombie's one thing, even a conscious one like you. But a live child … As I said, my son means more to me than anything. But there are lines no man should ever allow himself to cross. I couldn't turn a blind eye to what Dan-Dan was doing to the children. As far as we've fallen, I don't ever want to fall that far.'

'We will do all that we can to safeguard your son's future,' Dr Oystein says. 'Zhang will scour every inch of this ship in search of the Board members. Two have already been dealt with. If the others are still alive, we will find them. They will not be able to harm your boy once we have dealt with them.'

'Be careful what you promise, doc,' I mutter. 'I killed Lord Luca but the others got away. They had escape hatches in the hull which they were able to blow open. There were speedboats moored to the cruiser. Justin, Vicky and Dan-Dan all made it to freedom.'

Barnes's face whitens. He starts to tremble, then stops himself. 'I have to go,' he tells Dr Oystein.

'You can stay with us if you wish,' Dr Oystein says. 'We can hunt for them together.'

Barnes shakes his head. 'I don't know where they'll go. But I know where my son is. I'll try to get to the island and rescue him before it occurs to them to order his execution. They might not even be aware of my treachery. They weren't on deck when we boarded. I might have time to play with.'

'I wish you luck,' the doctor says.

'Thanks.' Barnes grimaces. 'I'm going to need it.' The hunter faces me and tries to think of something to say. In the end he simply shrugs. 'Like I said to you once before, it won't mean anything, I'm sure, but I'm sorry.'

'Me too,' I mumble. 'By the way,' I stop him before he leaves, 'where's Coley?'

Barnes manages a weak grin. 'He never would have gone for this. He didn't care about the children. I knocked him out and tied him up before I went to County Hall. I'll swing by and free him before setting off for the island. It's the end of our partnership, but I owe him that much.'

'Was he the one you were talking about the last time you came to see me?' I ask. 'When you said it was hard having to sacrifice someone you care about?'

'No,' Barnes smiles, warmly this time. 'I was talking about *you*.'

As I stare at him, he flips me a quick salute, then hurries out of the arena and heads off to try and save the one person in the world he truly loves, the boy whose life he risked in order to do what was right.

Barnes did something heroic and noble today. But if his son is killed as a result, he'll feel like the most miserable man alive. Everyone knows this isn't a world of black and white, but it's not a world of grey either. It's a world of hellish, soul-tormenting red, and Barnes is adrift on that choppy, bloodstained sea the same as the rest of us. I hope the ex-soldier finds his son and enjoys a bit of peace before his number is called.

But I wouldn't bet on it.

TWENTY-TWO

'We should get you back home as soon as possible,' Dr Oystein says. 'You need to spend a few weeks in a Groove Tube.'

'I've been in there a lot recently,' I sigh. 'One mauling after another. I must be the most unfortunate girl in the world.'

'Some might think otherwise,' the doc murmurs. 'If you had not been captured and forced to fight, and if you had not determined the conditions under which you would compete, how many children would Daniel Wood have killed? Some might say you are a hero.'

I snort. 'A zombie can't be a hero. We're monsters.'

Dr Oystein smiles. 'Then all I can say is that I wish there were more monsters like you in the world.'

We beam at each other. Then I shake my head before things get too mawkish. 'So how did it go down? Barnes came to you, told you what was happening and led you here?'

'In a nutshell, yes. He spotted the twins while they were gathering supplies. He approached them, explained the situation and asked for their help. They escorted him back to County Hall.'

'That's why Dr Oystein let us come on this mission,' Cian says proudly. He looks like the cat that not only got the cream but a mouse-flavoured stick to stir it with. 'If not for us, Barnes might never have found his way to County Hall, certainly not in time to save you.'

'We begged the doctor and Master Zhang to let us tag along and they agreed in the end,' Awnya says.

'I wouldn't say that we *begged*,' Cian grumbles.

'Why are you guys soaked to the skin?' I ask.

'We were part of the river team,' Awnya says.

'Most of us were,' Carl adds.

Now that I look closely, I see that all of the Angels in the room are wet, except for Dr Oystein and Rage.

'We could not attack from land,' Ashtat explains. 'The guards on deck had the surrounding area covered. They would have torn us to pieces with their rifles before we could close the gap.'

'The doc and I came back with Barnes,' Rage says. 'He tied us up, loose knots that we could wriggle out of. Pretended to the guards that he'd captured us.'

'We came at a time when he knew the Board would be watching you fight,' Dr Oystein says. 'We hoped to swoop on them when they were together, for the sake of Barnes's son.'

'While the guards were ogling the doctor and Rage,' Carl says, 'the rest of us scaled the far side of the cruiser. We'd swum here earlier in the day and were waiting just beneath the surface of the water.'

'We plugged our ears and noses and kept our mouths shut,' Cian says. 'Bobbed about there for more than an hour. It was cool!'

'I spotted a couple of speedboats while we were climbing,' Jakob says softly. 'I thought that was how the humans got to and from the ship. If I'd guessed they were for getaways, I would have torn holes in their hulls and sunk them.'

'How many of you came?' I ask.

'Most of the Angels,' Ashtat says.

'Every single Angel volunteered,' Shane says.

'I wasn't going to,' Rage sniffs, 'but I didn't want to be the odd one out. Would have looked bad.'

'You're all heart,' I grunt.

'We left some behind to take care of the place,' Carl says. 'Otherwise we're all here.'

'For *you*,' Dr Oystein whispers.

I shrug. 'What do you want me to do? Go round and thank everyone in person?'

'It wouldn't be a bad start,' Rage growls.

'Well, don't worry,' I laugh. 'I was planning to do just that. I might even hug a few of you beautiful buggers while I'm at it.'

'You see, B?' Dr Oystein says with a justified smile. 'You cannot be a true loner when you have so many people who love you.'

'*Love?*' I ask, arching an eyebrow at Rage.

Dr Oystein purses his lips. 'Well, maybe that is not *quite* the right word.'

'You don't have to hammer it home,' I tell him. 'I was wrong. I acted like an idiot. I'm sorry. I won't cut myself off from the rest of you again. I understand how lucky I am to have you guys on my side and I won't look to go it alone any more. Now, high-fives!'

And, like some overexcited kid after winning a cup final, I go around high-fiving everyone in the room, Dr Oystein, the twins, Carl, Jakob, Ashtat, Shane, even a cynically grinning Rage. And I don't feel the least bit embarrassed, because I'm not in the company of room-mates, colleagues or allies.

I'm with friends.

To be continued . . .